LUKEZILLA
BEATS THE GAME

BY KURTIS SCALETTA

CAPSTONE EDITIONS
a capstone imprint

Lukezilla Beats the Game is published by Capstone Editions,
an imprint of Capstone.
1710 Roe Crest Drive
North Mankato, Minnesota 56003
www.capstonepub.com

Library of Congress Cataloging-in-Publication Data is available on
the Library of Congress website.
ISBN: 978-1-68446-204-9 (hardcover)
ISBN: 978-1-68446-205-6 (eBook PDF)

Summary: In real life, Lucas is small and unathletic. But as Trunkzilla
in the online game Smashtown Frenzy, he's the biggest, toughest
fighter on the streets. No wonder he prefers games to reality! He
plans to spend all summer battling his way through the Smashtown
tournament with his team, but his parents have other plans for him:
volunteer work. Lucas is assigned to help Isaac, a retired librarian
who likes cats and detective novels. Then Isaac faces a health crisis,
and Lucas faces a moral dilemma. Lucas's actions start a spiral that
gets him thrown off his team, banned from Smashtown, and made
into a meme by internet haters. Then Lucas gets one last shot to prove
to his friends, his parents, and the whole internet that gaming means
the world to him—and that he'll never take the low road online or in
life.

Designed by Hilary Wacholz

Cover illustration by David Sossella

Printed and bound in China.
3322

For Byron, who inspired this book

PART 1
MINNEAPOLIS

CHAPTER 1

3 . . . 2 . . . 1 . . . BATTLE!

The text flashes across the screen and it's time to fight. The arena is a maze of streets and alleyways in a ruined city. I know this map by heart. I tap on the keys to send Trunkzilla storming up the center lane and around a corner. Then I see Vile the snake and Crusher the hyena. Both have a vicious bite. But once the other players see Trunky, their fighters freeze in their tracks. My elephant is the biggest, toughest fighter on the streets of *Smashtown*. Some noobs haven't even seen him before.

STOMP! One pound of Trunky's big elephant foot makes the ground tremble. Now Spry comes swinging in, pinching and punching our opponents with his little monkey fists. The player controlling him is Max, one of my best friends. Spry can do a lot of damage in a short amount of time. But he's squishy—meaning, easy to kill—so he backs off as soon as the ground stops quaking.

"It's your turn, Noah!" Tori's voice sounds over the battle noises.

Spike the rhino charges in to ramrod the wall of the enemies' fortress. He's played by Noah, my other best friend. The other team counters with Honeypie, a bee who coats the lane in honey and slows down our rhino. Spike struggles to free himself while their Caprina, a female ram—I know that makes no sense, but it's a game—charges down one of the side lanes toward our wall. Spry sprints back to meet her.

The honey-glue wears off, and now Spike can strike their fortress wall. You can see the wall cracking, but the snake gets a lick in and Spike's health drops. Pirrot flies over. She fans her plumage and all his health zooms back up. I stomp after the snake and get its tail, pinning it down. Meanwhile, Spry has forced Caprina to back off into the jungle.

"Second verse, same as the first!" Tori says. She's the player behind Pirrot, and our unofficial team leader. Spike resumes work on the wall. Spry keeps Caprina away from our wall. The snake squirts away, but I keep it from going after Spike. It's only a matter of time before we take down their fortress, but before the wall crumbles, my dad is there, laying his hands on the laptop and yanking it away.

"Wha—?"

"It's time to put the computer away for the night, Lucas," he says gravely.

"But, but, but . . . ," I sputter. "I was in the middle of a battle!"

"I've been warning you for fifteen minutes."

He probably has been. I tune out the rest of the world when I play *Smashtown Frenzy*. Besides that, I'm wearing headphones.

"Nooo!" I wail as Dad shuts the laptop and carries it away. Somewhere in another dimension, Trunkzilla has left the game.

• • •

I wake up in the middle of the night feeling like I've swallowed a ball of ice. I'm sure we've fallen off the leaderboard. In *Smashtown Frenzy*, you can only pick your opponent if both teams are on the leaderboard. Otherwise you're forced to play random matches, usually against low-ranking teams. When you're on the leaderboard, playing top teams, you can crank up a lot of points fast and stay there. But when you're playing noobs, it's a grind to get enough points to get back on the leaderboard. People on the gamer boards complain about it constantly. Of course, when you're *on* the leaderboard, it's pretty sweet.

We've been on the leaderboards a long time, because we've been playing practically since the game came out two years ago. We've racked up a lot of matches and are really good. But the game has suddenly exploded in popularity, and that's made it harder.

I try to talk myself down. We're probably still on the leaderboard. Even if we *did* fall off, we can get back on after a few dozen matches.

My fears give way to planning. Summer vacation is a week away. We'll be able to play all day, every day. We can crawl up the leaderboard until we're in the top one hundred. Maybe even the top ten. And number one? Well, *somebody* has to be number one.

• • •

"You look tired," Mom says at breakfast. I'm making toaster waffles. "Did you get enough sleep?"

"Nope."

"Hmm," she says. "You didn't find a screen and stay up late, did you?"

"No." Mom and Dad worry that I'm spending too much time "on screens." To them screens are all the same. Playing video games is the same as posting selfies is the same as bingeing on videos. It's like if someone said you were spending too much time "in water" and it didn't matter if you were drowning, swimming, or taking a bath.

"Can I make you an egg?" Mom asks. "Maybe you need more protein."

"I'm good." I pour cold syrup on my warm waffles.

"Anyway, we need to talk about your summer break," she says.

"We did talk about it. Dad is usually home and when he's not, I can be alone a few hours without burning down the house. I'm thirteen, Mom."

"I know you are. I'm not talking about day camps or babysitters. But we're worried you'll sit around and play games all day."

Which *is* my plan, so I say nothing.

"We want you to do something off-screen. A club or a sport. We want you to be well-rounded."

"I *do* play a sport. *Smashtown Frenzy*." I'm also round. Has she not looked at me recently?

4

"*Video games* are not *sports*."

"They are now. They're called e-sports. They're on TV and everything." I make a point with my sticky fork tines. "Some gamers make lots of money. Some become big stars."

"Hmm." Mom's *hmm* could take the skin off a peach.

"Mom, you always tell me I should follow my dreams."

"No, I don't," she teases. "Maybe you heard that at school?"

"Maybe, but it's still a good philosophy."

"Your teachers won't have to support you when you're a thirty-year-old with no job," she says. "You at least need a backup plan. And it's our job as parents to make sure you have one."

"Cyrus Popp's mom probably said that too."

"Is he an e-sports champ?"

"No, he has a gaming channel. He'll get a new game and play it live until he finishes, no matter how long it takes. Mom, he was once up for *three days* playing Death Race Four. He didn't sleep!"

"Why did he have to do it all at once?" she asks.

"Because that's his thing. It's a big deal to be the first one who beats the game. There are hundreds of gamers racing to do it. He always wins."

"So, you'll have the same competition," she says. "Probably more."

She's got a good point, so I change the subject.

"Can I please have my phone?" I can have the phone in the morning, but not the laptop. Not on school days. They started taking it away because I was waking up at three or four a.m. to play, then falling asleep in class. I couldn't help it. I would wake up thinking about *Smashtown* and couldn't get back to sleep.

"Sure," she says tiredly. She disappears for a moment and reappears with the phone. I open Tori's scoreboard app. You can't play *Smashtown Frenzy* on a phone, but she made an app so we can check our rankings. I don't know *how* she made it; Tori has mad skills. I type in my username and password because it's the only way to get to the leaderboard. I tell it I'm not a robot, and I'm in.

The 4LMNTs are holding on at number 893. If you're not impressed that we're in the top one thousand, you need to know the game has more than *a million* teams. Meaning we're in the top tenth of the top one percent, based on the total points we've racked up as a team. But we're sickeningly close to falling *off* the leaderboard, and we still have to get through the school day! That's seven hours when other teams will be surging ahead of us.

"I want a plan before the beginning of summer vacation," Mom says.

"Huh?" For a moment I think she means for staying on the leaderboard. But no. Mom doesn't know or care about that. "A plan for what?"

"For what you're going to do this summer besides play video games."

"Fine. OK." My mind races. Should I mow lawns for money? I hate pushing the mower up and down the street. Join a reading club at the library? It would be all fourth graders. Join park league sports? Don't make me laugh. If there's no *E* in front of it, sports are not for me. I used to play baseball, badly, but sports get supercompetitive once you're in middle school.

"We'll talk about it at dinner," Mom says. "You better have some ideas, or Dad and I will come up with a plan *for* you."

• • •

I am neither the biggest nor the toughest guy in the halls of Fremont Middle School. I'm squishier than a Play-Doh bunny, and have no fighting skills. But I am mostly invisible, which is a pretty great superpower when you're squishy.

Unfortunately, I am not invisible to Zach. He's a mid-level bully with untamed hair and a lot of freckles. He aspires to be a real bully, but he settles for targets like me, one of the only boys at Fremont Middle School who's shorter than he is. This morning he accidentally on purpose steps on my foot and says "Sorry" in that hollow, not-at-all-sorry way bullies use. I notice he's wearing a *Smashtown Frenzy* shirt. The starter characters are on it. Vile, Caprina, Honeypie, and Pango.

"Cool shirt," I tell him.

"What's that?" he asks testily.

"I said it's a cool shirt."

"What's wrong with my shirt?"

"Nothing. I love *Smashtown Frenzy*."

"I know. You and your nerd friends think you're so hot." He slams his locker door and departs. That's his game plan. Not to fight to the finish, but to score a few points and sneak away. He's a real-life scrub. Scrubs are battle gamers who take a few shots at the weakest enemies, but steer clear of the real battles.

Nobody wants somebody like that on their team.

That makes me feel a bit sorry for Zach. He mostly hangs out on the margin of a group of jocks who seem to barely know he's there. I've got the 4LMNTs. Individually, we're all decent players but nothing special. But *together*, we're on the leaderboard. And Zach must know it, even though none of us ever talk to him. Word has gotten around the school.

Speaking of the 4LMNTs, I see two of them down the hall. Noah is lanky and has tightly braided hair that would look cool on most kids but not on him. Max looks like every caricature of a computer nerd you've ever seen. He combs his hair down flat on his head and wears thick glasses. But his sister, Tori, is the real nerd. She's a computer wizard and a member of the robot club. She's an eighth grader at Fremont, but next year she's going to a STEM high school in the suburbs.

Max doesn't use his PC for anything but gaming. His glasses slide down his nose as he shakes his head at me.

"You quit in the middle of a battle!" he says.

Quitting in the middle of a match is the worst thing a gamer can do. Quitters are lower than scrubs.

"My dad grabbed the laptop. It was past my curfew. Did we lose the match?"

They both nod grimly.

"I got knocked out and they took our home base," Max tells me. "And they made fun of you for rage quitting."

"Gack," I sputter. Losing the match is bad enough, but noobs thinking I rage quit . . . that's unbearable. "We were *winning* before my dad took my laptop. Why would I rage quit if we were *winning*?"

They both shrug.

"Anyway, we'll play after school, right?" I say. "Get a few wins in to make up for it?"

"We can't," says Max. "Tori has a thing after school."

"A thing?" I ask.

"That's all she told me," he admits. "But we can both play all day tomorrow."

"Me too," Noah chimes in.

"What, we can't even play later tonight?"

"Tori has a thing. I told you."

"You said an after-school thing, not an all-night thing," I grumble. Fine. If Tori has a *thing*, she has a *thing*. But now any chances of staying on the leaderboard are smashed like a team of noobs under the broad feet of Trunkzilla.

• • •

We're off the leaderboard by the end of the day. It's the first time in a year that we've lost our place. I don't know by how far, because once you're off, you don't know your exact ranking. You just see your percentage. Like, we're still in the top one percent, but that could be two spots down, or it could be two hundred. Worse, I know we're still falling. Other teams are racking up points. We are not.

I pass the time by running one of my favorite *Frontiers* missions. *Smashtown Frenzy* has a spin-off game called *Smashtown Frontiers*. Both take place in a futuristic city where people have spliced their DNA with animals to give themselves superpowers, and both involve fighting. But in *Frontiers* you don't battle other players. You run a series of missions where you explore different parts of the city, fight non-player characters (NPCs), solve puzzles, search for loot, and rack up experience points (XP). They aren't called experience points in the game. They're called street cred. But everyone calls them XP anyway, because that's what they're called in most games. I'm way more into *Frenzy* now, but at least I can play *Frontiers* solo.

I finish a mission, but it's literally pointless. As in, you get no XP for repeating a mission. I take a break and go see what Cyrus Popp is up to.

Cyrus Popp is a Streamcast star who mostly plays games. He cracks everyone up with his commentary and reactions to things. He's got seventeen million subscribers. I read once that he's a millionaire. He also gets all the games and consoles free, and early, so it's a pretty awesome job. That's why he's my hero.

I tried to start my own channel on Streamcast, but I only have seventeen followers, and nobody's offered me anything. I need a gimmick. Cyrus has a gimmick: playing a game straight through in one session. He also has a cool Streamer name. If he'd stuck with his real name, Papakagis, *he* might have only seventeen followers.

My own username is Lukezilla, which'll do until I think of something better.

I notice the countdown timer on the corner of Cyrus's channel page. He's going live in five minutes! He usually goes live when there's a new game, but as far as I know, no big games are coming out any time soon. I wonder what the deal is? I click into the stream the second he goes live.

"Greetings, Cyborgs!" he says. He's wearing the long-billed fishing cap he always does, the bill slightly askew. He tugs the bill around to the back. "I'm as excited as a rooster in the henhouse to make this announcement on behalf of myself, Streamcast, and Kogeki Games. This summer I'll be hosting the first official *Smashtown Frenzy* Teen Tournament, which will be played live and in-person from coast to coast. I'll tell you some of the cities I'll be in. New York. Boston. Philadelphia. Washington, D.C. Atlanta. Miami. Detroit. Chicago. Minneapolis . . ."

He keeps going, explaining that the top teams from each city will face off in Chicago to name a national champion.

I am freaking out. He said Minneapolis. He said tournament. He said *Smashtown*. He said teen. Which means we can play in this tournament! Maybe even meet Cyrus Popp in person! And we have a real shot at winning. If we've been in the top thousand in the whole wide world, we must be the best team in Minnesota.

"You can find out all the details by following the link in the description of this video," he tells us. "I hope to see YOU on tour, and I'm so excited I'm stroking out!" He does this thing, blinking one eye and then the other, sticking his tongue out here and there, as if he's having a fit. It's one of his trademark bits. One time I did it in front of Mom when she said we were going to the pizza place with the arcade for dinner. Mom said strokes don't look like that, and neither do seizures, but who cares? It's funny.

This time it feels like it's not enough for how genuinely crazy-exciting this really is.

I'm about to text my friends, but my phone is already buzzing so hard it's going to shake off its protective case.

!!!!!! is all Max's message says, and he's right.

• • •

"So," Mom says at dinner. "Have you thought of what you want to do this summer?"

"Yes!" I say but then realize she won't want to hear about the *Smashtown* tournament. She's asking for my nongaming plans. "I mean, yeah, but I couldn't think of anything."

"I've got something you can look at," Dad says. He's on his laptop, tapping away with his left hand and eating with his right. Usually there are no screens at the dinner table, but apparently this is an exception. He turns the computer so I can see the screen. Youth Service Corp America, it says. I imagine kids in uniforms marching around with flags.

"It's for teenage volunteers," he explains. "They match up kids with opportunities."

"Like what?"

"All kinds of stuff. Planting trees. Picking up litter."

"Ugh. Bees and sunburns."

"Most likely," Dad admits. "If you want something indoors, you can . . . uh . . . be a kitchen helper at Helping the Homeless?" He gives me a hopeful look.

"I do have lots of experience washing dishes," I say. We have a small kitchen, and no room for a dishwasher, so I do them every night by hand. I decide I don't need any more experience. "What else is there?"

"Walking dogs at the animal shelter?"

"He's scared of dogs," Mom reminds him, which isn't fair. I'm only scared of big dogs.

"Oh yeah." Dad keeps scrolling through the options.

"You should do something you're interested in," Mom says.

"I don't think they need anyone to play video games," Dad says.

"Oh, come on Nick. He *does* have other interests," Mom says.

"No, I don't," I tell her.

Dad types "video games" into the search and hits the enter key.

"Nothing for *video* games," he says. "But there are matches for *games*. Look at this. You can be a senior sitter."

"A what?"

"Spend time with elderly people," Dad explains. "Play board games, do puzzles. Go out into the community. Listen to their boring stories—"

"It does not say *boring*," Mom interrupts.

"Right," Dad says. "Sorry for editorializing. Anyway, Lucas, it does say you might do light chores. But mostly the seniors want companionship."

"You do like puzzles and board games," Mom says. "You used to do them with us."

"Yeah . . ."

"And you're a good companion," Dad adds. "I enjoy your company."

"Hmm." I think it over. I don't really know any old people.

Dad's dad lives in Brazil, and his mother died when I was a baby. *His* grandfather moved to Brazil from Italy and married a Brazilian woman, then his dad came to the U.S. to go to college and married an American but went back to Brazil after they divorced. Anyway, I'm really not connected to that side of the family.

Mom's mom, who we call Mammaw, lives in Nashville. We almost never see her because she and Mom had a falling out. And Mom doesn't know *her* dad because Mammaw was a single mom. So I don't really know *that* side of the family either. It isn't fair.

The truth is, I've always kind of wanted the grandma/grandpa stuff other kids talk about. A grandma who makes cookies or a grandpa who takes me golfing and lets me drive the cart. Or maybe a grandpa who makes pie and a veteran grandma who teaches me archery and tells me war stories. I'm open-minded.

"How do I sign up?"

CHAPTER 2

Which is how I end up on the front porch of a small house on the first Monday of summer vacation. The house is a washed-out gray. There are no other houses on the street; it's all alone in a row of small businesses.

I'd noticed it before from the on-ramp to Interstate 94. I'd always wondered who lived here, a lone house amid all the machine shops and storage facilities, perched on a hill with a collapsing wire fence around it. Now I know. His name is Isaac Biddle.

It's actually my second trip here. The first time I came with Mom and Wendy, the match coordinator from Senior Sitters. But it's the first time I'm here by myself. I lock my bike to the railing on the porch, which is sagging and could probably be torn off with a good pull. I ring the buzzer and wait. Nobody comes to the door. I know Isaac is home because I can hear a voice blaring even over the clanging from the Norseman Metalworking Shop next door, and the rush of cars on the interstate. At first I think it's the radio, but then I'm not sure.

It's one voice going on and on with no interruptions.

I bang on the door again.

"Mr. Biddle?"

I'm about to turn and walk away when the voice inside goes quiet. A moment later I see wrinkly eyes squinting at me through the pane of glass on the porch door, and the door creaks open.

"What are you selling?" he asks.

"Nothing. I'm with Senior Sitters. I was here a couple days ago, remember?"

"Oh right. The boy." He opens the door and lets me into the foyer.

Isaac is black. He's shrunken the way old people often are, with a fringe of white hair around his bald head. He wears glasses and has a sweater on, even though it's the middle of June. He cracks a grin, and I see he is still doing fine for teeth, unless they are false ones.

"How're you doing?" I ask.

"Fair to middlin'," he says.

"You sure read a lot," I tell him, looking at some books on a small table. *The Case of the Green Gauntlet* and *Coffin Season*. Mysteries. A chubby mostly black cat is curled up next to them. We have never had a pet so I'm not sure what to do. I pat him on the head. The cat looks up at me with an annoyed expression. I back away.

"I used to read," he says. "I don't see well enough anymore even for the big-print ones, but a friend brings me books on tape." He gestures at a machine, which must be the source of the voice I heard through the door. "It was her idea to sign up for a kid to come over."

"Oh yeah? It was my parents' idea I do this." So neither of us *really* wants to be a companion. Maybe I can make it quick and go home to game. But Wendy from Senior Sitters said Isaac might need help around the house. "Do you need me to, um, do anything?"

"Maybe the cat boxes? It's hard for me to take the stairs, and even harder to bend over. Yolanda used to do them. That's the lady who brings me books. But now she's got a new knee and . . . well, she can't do the stairs anymore either." He gestures toward the kitchen, where I can see heaps of dirty dishes in the sink. "The steps are through there." I see another cat—this one a long-limbed orange stripy one—walking across the counter in the kitchen. "Grab a bag from the railing. You can change the boxes if you want. I scooped them a couple days ago but it's been about a month since they've been changed. So, uh, you'll need a new bag of litter. It's inside the back door. I have it delivered. I can take those stairs about once a day but I can't carry a twenty-pound bag."

"Uh . . . sure." I see the plastic grocery bags wadded up and stuffed into the railing. I grab a few, then pick up the bag and haul it down the steep, narrow stairway. The basement is unfinished. It has a concrete floor and whitish walls marked by water stains. Everything smells wet and old. And there are the cat boxes. Two of them, clumpy and poopy, with sand kicked out to the floor. There is a *lot* of poop. How many cats does Isaac have?

I look from box to bag, and bag to box, trying to figure out how to do this without throwing up. I finally just slide one box into a bag, tilt it up, and let the, um, solids pour out. I give the box a couple whaps to knock out the clumps stuck to the bottom. Then I do it with the other box. Second verse, same as the first, as Tori would say. I refill the boxes and carry the full, heavy bags upstairs and outside to the garbage bins

"Did you wash out the boxes after you emptied them?" Isaac calls from the living room.

"Um . . . yeah." I make a note to do that next time.

"Want to listen to the story with me?" Isaac asks. "I rewound it to the beginning for you." Since he went to the trouble, I nod and sit down.

He hits play and the deep-voiced man starts up again.

It's about a surfer detective named Ross Cooper. The author describes him as tan and fit and having a flashing smile. He's helping a woman look for her missing husband. Apparently, her hubby popped out of their motel room for ice on their honeymoon and never came back. The detective suggests the groom got cold feet, but the bride says no, he left the room wearing only shorts and didn't take his wallet.

The surfer detective wanders around this touristy beach town talking to people, looking for clues. He realizes he's being followed by a beefy Italian guy.

Don't run, the detective thinks. *That's what they expect.*

So instead of running or trying to escape, he turns around and walks straight at the guy following him. Now it's the fat guy's turn to flee.

Isaac shuts off the machine.

"Time for lunch," he announces.

"Huh? Already?" I glance at my phone. It's after eleven. Early for lunch, but later than I thought.

"Do you like olives?" he asks.

"Maybe?" I tell him. "We never get olives on pizza, so I'm not sure if I like them."

"Might as well try them," he says and disappears into the kitchen. I guess he's going to feed me? I am kind of hungry, but I expected cookies, not olives. I'm beginning to think driving a golf cart isn't going to happen with Isaac either.

I feel a tap on my shoulder and I nearly jump out of my skin. It's the stripy cat. He crawls down my chest and settles in my lap. I timidly touch his head, softer than I did with the black one. This cat shuts his eyes and purrs.

"Well, I'll be." Isaac is back with a plate. He shoves some books out of the way so he can set it on the table next to me. "Petey doesn't like most people."

"Really?"

"And he's an excellent judge of character," Isaac says.

I pick up a sandwich half, which is dark brown bread with white and green goo on the inside. I take a bite. The bread is bitter. The inside is creamy and salty and unlike anything I've ever tasted.

"Do you like it?" Isaac asks.

"I do," I tell him. I take another bite to prove it, keeping my lap perfectly still so I don't disturb the cat. Isaac hits play on the audiobook and the story continues. The surfer detective guy returns home and finds a message from the woman—his client—and she's hysterical. Somebody broke into her room. She describes him. The surfer detective realizes it's the same guy who was following him earlier!

My phone buzzes. The noise scares Petey, who gouges me with his back claws as he springs away.

Coming over soon? the message says. It's Noah. We were supposed to get together this afternoon to game. I glance up and realize Isaac has fallen asleep.

OMW, I tap out. I get up and turn off the tape player.

"Thanks for coming," Isaac murmurs as I'm about to open the door. "See you tomorrow?"

"Right. Sure. See you tomorrow."

• • •

"Where *were* you?" Max wants to know. He's waiting with Noah on the front porch of my house. "We were supposed to meet at your house after lunch."

"Sorry. But it's still *technically* after lunch." I fumble through my pocket for my back door key. We'd played a lot over the last week, but with the tournament coming up it never feels like enough. "My dad is home. You could have knocked."

"We did. He didn't hear us."

I unlock the door and we go into the kitchen. I hear my dad bumping around downstairs where he has a little office set up. He was laid off a few months ago and has been looking for work ever since. He had a good job, something to do with databases. Dad says there aren't a lot of jobs working with that kind of database, so he's had to apply for jobs working with other databases. He gets lots of first interviews and no second interviews.

Noah runs off to the bathroom. Max helps himself to a bag of wavy potato chips and a soda from the fridge. We're like that in one another's houses.

"Where's Tori?" I ask him.

"She's at home," he says around a mouthful of chips. "She says to text when we're ready and she'll log in."

"Want to text her now? That way she'll be ready when we are."

"Fine." He pulls out his phone and taps out a message.

We set up at the kitchen table. We have a power strip in there so everyone can plug in. A few minutes later we're all logged in except Tori.

"Where is she?" I ask Max. He shrugs.

"She's my sister, not my conjoined twin."

"It seems like she's bailing on us all the time," I complain. "The tournament is in ten days!"

"I know, I know," he says. "Why are you yelling at me?"

"Sorry. It's super frustrating."

"I'm sure she'll play. She said she would."

"We can play *Frontiers* while we wait," Noah suggests.

"I don't want to get sucked into a mission," I tell him. "We have to practice for the tourney. And get back on the leaderboard." We never did fight our way back on, but we've been thinking way more about the tournament than the leaderboard.

"Come on!" pleads Noah. "One quick mission?"

"Fine. But we're quitting the second Tori gets on."

"How about Crosswise Corners?" Noah suggests.

"Sure. I love that one." It's a maze of tight alleyways plagued with enemies, but also full of loot.

"Pick your fighters for the challenge." Noah narrows his eyes at me. "That means no Trunkzilla."

"Why not?"

"We don't need a tank," he says. "There's no open ground and no melee battles. You'll have to be nimble and be able to jump and climb." He's right. Trunky's usual pros won't help, and he'll have some cons.

"Fine." I sigh and look through my other options. I've played them all. But I feel a kinship with Trunky I can't explain. It's more than game strategy. When I'm Trunky, I'm *in* the game. When I'm any other character, I'm *playing* the game.

I finally settle on Mustina. She's a badger assassin—fierce, but not too squishy.

"I can't believe you picked a girl," Max teases.

"What of it? She's good." Max usually doesn't say stuff like that.

"But sometimes they're not reliable," he mutters. I guess he's also mad at Tori for bailing on us.

• • •

"Don't bolt down your food," Mom says at dinner. "Tell us how today went."

"I ran a mission with Max and Noah. Tori went AWOL."

"I mean with Mr. Biddle," she says.

"Oh yeah." Several hours of *Smashtown* have wiped Isaac out of my mind. "He's all right."

"What did you do?"

"Cleaned the cat boxes. Listened to a book on tape about a surfing detective."

"Ross Cooper?" Dad says.

"You've heard of him?"

"There was a TV show in the Eighties," Dad says. "I watched it sometimes."

"In any case, that sounds pleasant," Mom says. That's an old person word. Kids don't say anything is *pleasant*. But it is the perfect word. It wasn't exactly *fun* to hang out with Isaac and his cats, but it was pleasant.

• • •

I go to Isaac's every morning. I scoop cat boxes, take out the recycling, and wash dishes. Then I listen to part of an audiobook with Petey in my lap, eat a cheese and olive sandwich, and spend the rest of the day smashing noobs. It's not a bad life.

But when Wendy calls from the Senior Sitters place to check in, she makes a "Hmmm" noise like she's not completely satisfied with my senior sitting.

"That's all you do?" she asks. "Listen to audiobooks?"

"It's what he likes," I tell her. "And I do help out, especially with the cats."

"And I'm sure he appreciates it," she says sincerely. "But it's our hope that the program will help people like Isaac get out and into the community. It's what our funders want."

I remember something about "community" in the job description, but figured it would only be if the senior wanted that.

"I can't exactly *make* him leave the house—" I start to argue, but she cuts me off.

"He might need a little prodding is all," she says. "Suggest an outing. He's eligible for Metro Mobility, so you two can go anywhere you want in the city. And we can pay admission to either of the zoos and most of the museums in town."

"All right. I'll prod." But I wonder where in the city would a guy like Isaac want to go?

• • •

"What's in the bag?" Isaac asks me the next day.

"My computer," I tell him. We're practicing at Max and Tori's house later. Usually I swing by my house to grab it, but with the tournament in five days, we want to squeeze in every possible minute of practice.

"They keep making them smaller and smaller," he says in wonder. "My first computer took up practically my whole desk. That was 1980."

"No kidding? What did you do?" For some reason I've never thought to ask what he did when he still had a job. Most people didn't have computers back then. "Were you some kind of scientist?"

"Ha. No, I was a legal librarian," he says.

"There are illegal ones?"

"I mean I worked at a law library," he explains with a laugh. "We were one of the first professions to use computers. It sure made my job a lot easier. But what does a boy need a portable computer for in the middle of summer?"

"To play an online battle game called *Smashtown Frenzy*."

"What? I didn't understand any of that," he says.

"Well, you've probably heard of *Smashtown*? Because they've been making games since the early 2000s. *Smashtown Brawl, Smashtown Melee* . . ."

"Nope." He shakes his head.

"You've heard of video games? You've, like, walked by arcades?"

"Sure. *Pac-Man Fever*." He waves at me with one finger. "That was a big one, right?"

"It was called *Pac-Man*, but yeah. Games have changed a lot since then. The game play is way more complicated. There's usually a whole wide world you explore. Like, *Smashtown* takes place in a big futuristic city. And a lot of games are online, meaning people can log in from anywhere in the world and play together, or against each other."

"Can I see?" he asks in a hush. "That sounds amazing."

"Sure." I push some books out of the way and set the laptop on the coffee table. I sit on the floor while he relaxes into his favorite chair and leans forward until he's about two inches from the screen. I forget that he's going blind.

I realize I can't show him *Smashtown*. He doesn't have internet access. But I do have some of the game play video I captured for my Streamcast channel, so I show him that. My first video shows Trunkzilla running through a mission in *Smashtown Frontiers*. Isaac watches in fascination.

"This is mission mode," I tell him. "And *this* is battle mode." I open another video. We watch our team take down some opponents. It's been my most popular video, with fifty-something views. I still have a long way to go to reach Cyrus Popp numbers. "The big difference is that every one of these characters is a different human player."

"And you don't have to be in the same room?"

"You don't have to be in the same *country*. Everything is online. I'm on a team called the four elements, but we spell it numeral four, capital L, capital M, capital N, capital T. That's for Lucas, Max, Noah, and Tori. Get it?"

He nods. "Pretty clever."

"But it's got a double meaning, because the game itself has four elements. There are tanks, cannons, assassins, and support. I'm the tank. It's not a real tank, it's slang for the biggest, toughest defender." I see his eyes glazing over. "Anyway, we're going to be in a tournament so we have to practice." I shut the computer and shove it back into my bag.

"Sounds like you spend a lot of time playing these games," he says.

"Yep."

"I'll bet your parents don't like it?"

"Not much, no." I wonder if *he's* going to lecture me.

"My mother thought I spent too much time reading," he says.

"What? That doesn't sound like any parent I ever heard of!"

"Too much time reading *trash*, that is," he says with a wry smile. He switches to a high voice and wags his finger, mimicking a long-ago scolding. "You and your lurid detective novels! You could at least read improving books."

"Sounds like my mom." I laugh. "Except she's happy if I'm reading anything, as long as I'm off a screen."

"The more things change, the more they stay the same," he says.

I remember that I'm supposed to prod him to go on an outing.

"Would you ever want to . . . like, go somewhere?" I ask him. "Wendy says—"

"Yeah, I know what Wendy says," he mutters. "She called me too. My mother's long gone but I still have people yapping at me to do more with my life."

"Uh . . ."

How much prodding should I do? I don't want him to think I'm just one more person yapping at him.

"It's scary to go out there when you can't see four feet in front of you," he admits. "I used to go out, but that's why I don't anymore."

"But plenty of people can't see at all. They manage."

"I know, I know." He draws in a big breath. "I was training Sam to be a seeing eye cat, but he only ever dragged me into the kitchen for treats."

I laugh.

"So, should we listen to our lurid detective novel?" he asks.

"Sure," I say.

So we do. Petey the cat settles back into my lap and lets me scratch his ears.

We're on to another Ross Cooper book. In this one Ross is trying to track down a guy who owes his client money. It turns out the missing guy is a gambler and had to borrow the money to pay off the mob, but Ross suspects he was murdered anyway. We break for sandwiches. Olives and cream cheese on dark bread again. The Isaac Biddle special. I've decided I really like them. The mobsters nab Ross and bring him on this houseboat-slash-lair where the boss lives. They want to know who he is and why he's sniffing around. Ross knows they're going to let him go; otherwise they wouldn't have blindfolded him. *It's a game of cat and mouse*, Ross thinks. *But the mouse has an advantage if he can think like a cat.*

My phone starts buzzing. I guess that it's Max, telling me to get over there so we can practice.

"I better go," I tell Isaac.

"Oh!" he says. "I'll pause the story for you."

"Thanks." I really do want to know how Ross is going to get out of this jam.

"And let's do something out of the house, next time," he says. "Make Wendy happy."

"OK. Do what?"

"I have an idea" is all he says.

"Great. Now I have two mysteries waiting for me."

He holds up one finger and nods at my joke.

My phone buzzes again. Max again. What *is* his problem? I grab my computer bag and hurry outside. I pedal as hard as I can to Max's house. When he lets me in, he has a serious expression.

"Hey, Lucas." It's like he's welcoming me to a funeral.

Noah's there, looking equally down. But before I can ask what's going on, I see Zach sitting on the couch. Zach the low-level bully. Zach the scrub. Zach the fight-picker.

"Hey," he says, which is the nicest thing he's ever said to me.

"What's up?" I ask Max, clearly meaning "What is *he* doing here?"

"Tori quit the team," he tells me.

CHAPTER 3

"She *what?*"

"She quit the team," Max says again. His voice is flat and unemotional.

"She doesn't want to be in the tournament?!"

"She's joined a new team. All ninth graders. That's *why* she quit. I think she went on practicing with us until she knew the new team was good enough for the tournament."

So that explained her bailing on us again and again. She was with another team. I feel utterly betrayed.

I need to sit down, but the only place to sit is on the couch between Max and Zach, and I don't want to sit next to Zach. He might punch me or something.

"So what are *we* going to d—" I start to say, and stop. I know what we're going to do. We're replacing Tori with Zach. I give him a look. He gives me a look back, his mouth twisted into a smirk. *What are you going to do about it?* his look seems to say.

"I saw him at the library playing *Smashtown* on the

computer," Max explains. "I've heard he's good."

"Fine." What choice do we have? The local tournament is in less than a week. I plop down on the couch next to Zach. "Welcome to the 4LMNTs," I tell him.

"Shouldn't we be the 4LMNZ?" he asks. "It's not much different, but Z for Zach."

"No!" the rest of us answer all at once.

"You see, we already registered the team name," Max explains.

I'm already annoyed, but it gets worse.

"I don't want to be a bird!" he complains when we suggest he play as Pirrot.

"You don't have to be Pirrot, but we do need a support," Noah says.

"What are the other choices?" Zach asks. I sigh. If he doesn't know which are the support characters . . .

"Minerva. She's an owl," Max says. "Bizzard, who's a. . . ."

"A buzzard, I know," says Zach. "I hate buzzards."

"Everything in the third column," I tell him, pointing at the grid on the selection screen.

"They're all birds! I don't want to be a bird!"

"There is a bat," I offer. "And a flying squid." But you need to be at a high level to unlock them, and I have a feeling Zach isn't there yet. You unlock one character every time you level up. Trunky is level forty. They saved the best for last.

"I'm always Pango," he says stubbornly.

"Pango is a tank," Noah explains. "We already have a tank."

"What's a tank?" Zach asks.

I roll my eyes so hard it hurts.

"It's the lead defender," Noah says, with the patience of a kindergarten teacher.

"So why can't we have two tanks?"

"Because only noobs do that," Max interjects. "They all want to be tanks because they're the biggest, toughest-looking characters. But they aren't great attackers."

"The assassin is the one who can run in and take out the best enemies," Noah adds. "The cannons do a lot of damage, but their attacks aren't focused. They hurt everyone around them, even their own teammates if they get too close. Cannons are good for bringing down the wall. Support characters have special moves that give your team a boost or hurt your opponents. They can always fly, because they need to get around. That makes them good for the team leader because they can keep an eye on the big picture."

Zach nods. "I've heard those terms but wasn't sure what they meant."

"You don't see them in the game itself," Noah says generously. "It's gamer slang. Anyway, our biggest weakness is that Spry and Spike are squishy. We need a healer. That's why Tori was Pirrot. Her support is health."

"Why can't Luke be the bird?" Zach says sulkily.

"Lucas," I correct him. I may be Lukezilla but I'm never Luke. Once you're Luke, everyone's like: "Luke, I'm your father." It's a bad road to go down.

"Lucas has unlocked the best tank in the game," Noah says. "So unless you . . ." Zach looks poised to storm out. ". . . Unless *he* wants to switch, he'll be the tank," Noah finishes and gives me a begging look. Great. Now it's up to me. If I don't give in, Zach could leave, and then we won't even have a team.

"How about you be that badger you like?" Max whispers to me. "If you take over as lead assassin, *I* can be support. It's the best role for the team leader, anyway."

"Whoa, you're leader now?" Noah asks.

"Somebody has to be," says Max with a shrug.

I feel queasy. *I'm Trunkzilla*, I want to shout, and prove it with a big foot stomp. But a smaller, strategic voice is already whispering to me. A tank is really the best role for a noob. All Zach has to do is wade in and take damage. He won't have to be as skilled. Meanwhile, support is the worst role for a noob. Support players need to be quick, alert, and selfless. Support players need to read the map and figure out what the other team is up to.

"Let's play that way today," Max says gently. "See how it goes?"

"Fine." I will be the badger. I will let Max call himself team leader. I will let Zach be on my team and be the tank. I will do all that because I want to play in the tournament and meet my hero. Even if it feels like I betrayed a real friend by giving up Trunkzilla. I put on my best Cyrus Popp impression and use of one his favorite phrases.

"Let's smash some noobs."

• • •

I groan when I see Zach's Pango is wearing a flak jacket and wraparound mirrored shades. You can trade loot from missions for those skins or spend real money on them. It's a free-to-play game, so the way Kogeki makes their money is in-game purchases and merchandise. Which must make them a fortune, since every other kid is wearing a *Smashtown* T-shirt or carrying a *Smashtown* backpack. I myself have dumped a lot of allowance on vinyl figurines. But I don't bother with skins. None of us 4LMNTs do, because skins don't give you an advantage in the game. I'd rather people marvel at my skill than my bling.

It turns out Zach is not as bad as I feared. He does have annoying habits, like shouting "Whoop!" when anybody takes out anybody. But he has the moves down and understands his role. He's not the scrub I thought he'd be. He digs in and fights.

In one match we face some very aggressive players. They've got two Leothrawl, which are lion assassins, and two Kwill, which are exploding porcupine cannons. They move fast, crossing into our territory before we're quite ready.

"Pango, guard the wall," Max says. Zach does so without arguing, which surprises me. The lions start slashing at the giant armored pangolin, but he doesn't budge, even with his health meter dwindling.

"Mustina, use your sneak attack," Max says.

"Stealth slice," I remind him. I trigger it; my badger scampers behind their assassins and slashes their behinds. I do it again and again, stealth slice to get behind them, slash. It takes good timing to slash and dodge. One does gouge me with a claw, but I survive the battle and take out both lions. Max's Pirrot heals

Mustina and Pango with a flare of plumage.

Before we take our next move, the Kwill curl up and detonate, blasting us and our wall with their spines. They do lots of damage to us but also take out each other. The message comes up that we've won the match. We didn't take their base or even enter their territory, but the game is over because we wiped out all four of their fighters before any could respawn.

GGNR, one of their player types into the text chat. Good game, no rematch. It's a sore loser thing to say. It's the next thing to rage quitting.

"Noobs," Zach says with a barking laugh. "They didn't even have a tank."

"Nah, you need serious XP to unlock those characters," Noah tells him. "They're experimenting. Seeing if they can get quick wins by being super aggressive. It probably works against most teams, but not us."

"It *would* have worked if you hadn't healthed up Pango and Mustina," Noah says with a nod to Max. "And if Mustina hadn't worked the stealth move so well. And if Pango hadn't hung in there taking the damage." He nods at me and Zach in turn. Acting like the team leader, giving us all our props. Maybe this new lineup will work.

"It proves we can beat a good team," I say. Zach is pretty good, but I'm not ready to tell him that yet.

"We're going to smash those noobs!" Max says, impersonating Cyrus Popp.

"I'm so excited I'm stroking out!" Zach does the Cyrus Popp bit, poking his tongue in and out, winking and blinking.

It cracks us all up. I'm not starting to like Zach, exactly, but I'm beginning to think the two of us can be on the same team.

• • •

"Today is the day," Isaac tells me the moment I walk in Friday morning. I don't have to ask what it's the day for. He's dressed to go out. He's wearing one of those plaid caps old men like, and is holding a wooden cane.

"Uh . . . OK." I'm supposed to practice with the guys, but I can text Max. "Where are we going?"

"I'm going to show you something," he says. "Come on, we can catch the Twenty-Two in five minutes."

"The what?"

"It's a bus." He follows me out and locks the door. "I need you to be my eyes," he says. "Help me cross the street and make sure we get on the right bus."

"Sure. You know, Wendy at the Senior Sitters says you're eligible for—"

"I know, I can take the old people van. But the Twenty-Two drops us off right in front of where we're going."

We cross one busy street to catch a bus going south. I make sure we're on the right bus, and Isaac uses a transit card to pay for both of us. We sit in the front. There are only a few riders this time of day.

As we ride, I text Max that I'll be late.

WHAT? HOW LATE? He asks in all caps.

IDK, I write back.

I can get why he's stressed, but what can I do?

The bus rumbles through downtown, then continues south. Isaac pulls the yellow cord when the driver announces that the next stop is the university.

"I need you to find something called the Anderson Library," he says. I pull up a map on my phone and enlarge the campus. "We can go through this building right here," I tell him. "It looks like all the buildings are connected."

We walk slowly through the first building. I'm glad for the air conditioning. Isaac peers around.

"Where are we?"

"The Law School." I noticed the sign over the door when we walked in.

"It's all new," he says. "Nothing's the same."

"Huh?"

"I went here," he said. "Then I worked here for thirty, thirty-five years, I guess. More or less. At the library."

"Do you want to go in and say hi to people?"

"Oh, nobody there will remember me. I retired almost twenty years ago."

We head through some connected buildings, down an elevator, through some double doors, and wind up in a little open area with glassed-in cases. We're in the entryway of something called the Charles Babbage Institute. They all have old-style computers. Some are *really* old.

Isaac walks right up to the glass and puts his face to it, trying to see. "It must be that big red blob," he says. "There weren't many red computers. What does the placard say?"

"'U.B.I.Q. terminal,'" I read aloud. "'Used for computer-assisted legal research. LexisNexis 1979. Donated by Isaac Biddle.' Hey! That's you!"

"Yep, that was mine," he says. "When I first got it, I was the egghead computer whiz. By the time I retired, I was an old stick-in-the-mud who didn't want an e-mail account. I never saw the point to having a computer at home."

"Wow. Did you ever play games on it?" I know they had games from the beginning of the computer age.

"No, but it sure made my job easier. I could search for law cases instead of pulling down massive books."

"Why did you decided to be a legal librarian?"

"I didn't *decide* so much as end up as one," he says. He takes a few steps and sits down on a bench. I guess all the walking and standing has taken something out of him. I sit next to him, scanning the huge old computers in the display case.

"My mother expected me to become a lawyer," he tells me. "I even got a law degree, but I didn't have enough ambition to actually practice law. People work eighty-hour weeks in that field. But you know, not everybody needs to be a hotshot lawyer saving the world. I was lucky to have a job I liked, where people treated me with respect. I could leave at five o'clock so I could go home and do what I loved."

"Read mysteries?" I guess.

"Not *only* read mysteries. I used to *watch* mysteries too. Back when I could see."

"Ha. That's like me with my games," I say. "I want to be a gamer, but Mom thinks I'll need a backup plan. When she's, you know, yapping at me." I use the word he did a few days ago.

"Mothers aren't always wrong," he says. "Doing legal research was kind of like being a sleuth. It suited me just fine."

"Yeah, I guess I do need a backup plan." There's no way I'll tell Mom about this conversation. She'll say she told me so.

"I was lucky to get a good job," Isaac says. "You know, when I was a little boy, the newspaper still had different job listings for white people and black people."

"Wow. Really?"

"Really. And this was in Minneapolis, Lucas. Not Birmingham. But then came the war and Jackie Robinson. By the time I was looking for work, newspapers didn't do that anymore, but employers were still *thinking* it. You better believe it. I applied to a hundred different law firms before I found this job. I was applying for jobs like law clerk, paralegal."

"But you had a whole law degree!"

"Yep," he says. "I ended up in a pretty good place, even if it wasn't my dream."

"What was that?"

He doesn't answer. He looks lost in thought for a while, then says again, "Mothers aren't always wrong."

"Do you want to have lunch somewhere?" I ask. "Or go home?"

"I like home," he says.

• • •

"So, we've been thinking," Mom says at dinner, which is my favorite: chili dogs and tater tots.

Uh-oh. I drop the tot I was about to shove in my mouth.

Nothing good ever comes of conversations that begin with: "So, we've been thinking." I now wonder if the chili dogs are a way of softening the blow of whatever it is they've been "thinking."

"We haven't had a vacation in a long time," she says. "That's because money is tight, but my old friend Debbie Kane . . . you remember her? She was my college roommate and lives in Rochester?"

"I remember." Debbie has frizzy hair and two big barky dogs.

"She said we can use her cabin next week. For the whole week!"

"Where is it?"

"Grand Rapids. It's right on a lake. It'll be so nice."

"Does it have Wi-Fi?"

"That's the best part," she says. "We feel like we can *all* use a week off the grid. No work e-mail or Facebook for me. No job searches or discussion boards for your dad. We'll enjoy fresh air, nature, and family time."

"That's *not* the best part, it's the *worst* part!" I mutter. It's like telling me we'll all have a refreshing break from oxygen. "What about the tournament?"

"We won't leave until after the city tournament," Mom says.

"It's a chance for you to recover if you lose." Dad says. "*If*," he repeats, seeing the look on my face. "And if you win, which you probably will, it's a much-needed rest before the national tournament in August." The top four teams from every local tournament move on to a national tournament in Chicago.

"But we'll need to practice!"

"Max and Tori won't be here anyway," Mom says. "I saw their mom at the store. She told me."

She's right. The Zellers go to their own cabin every Fourth of July.

"Tori's not on the team anymore," I tell her. But that doesn't matter. Without Max there's no practice.

"The break from games and the internet will be good for you," Mom says.

I remember what Isaac said earlier that day. *Mothers aren't always wrong.* Not *always*, but definitely *sometimes*, including *this time*.

• • •

Dad drives me downtown Thursday morning and drops me off near the convention center. Outside there are already hundreds of teens. Most of them are older than us. Guys with long hair and skateboards tucked under their arms. Guys with buzz cuts and camo shorts. Girls with lip rings and hair dyed in crazy colors.

Lots of kids have had official team T-shirts made with their team name and a logo. Some names are obvious, like NE_Mpls. Others are clever or mysterious, like CTRaffers, Snarknados, and TheVB88s. My favorite is MuchTeam! with a drawing of Doge, the famous dog meme. I wish our team had thought of team T-shirts.

The mood in the air is awesome. It may be a competition, but everyone here loves gaming and that connects us. Kids are excited and happy, chatting, and goofing around. It's fun to be a part of this.

I see a sign directing the gamers to the lower level and jump on a jammed escalator. I feel a whack in the back of my head as soon as I get off. I whirl around and see Zach giving me his classic *What are you going to do about it?* look. But then he offers a fist to bump.

"I don't like it when you do that," I tell him, holding back my fist.

"I was trying to get your attention." He shrugs. "So are you ready to . . ." We finish it together. ". . . *smash some noobs?*"

I let him fist bump, which is better than a whack to the back of the head.

In front of the escalator a long table is set up with a sign. Sign in here. Entire team must be present. So we wait, trying to stand where Max and Noah will see us as they come off the escalator. "We're gonna smash some noobs!" Zach says a couple more times, not understanding that once was enough.

Max and Tori finally find us. Tori says hi guiltily, and scoots away to find her team. I haven't seen her since she ditched us, and want to let her have it, but not in the middle of a crowded hallway. Besides, we have to stay focused.

Max waves at Noah, who's coming down the escalator. We sign in and get handed yellow papers with our first two match times and table assignments. The first one is in forty minutes.

A crowd has already gathered around the doors of Hall B and Hall C, waiting to get in. At last the security guards throw open the doors, and the mob surges into the hall, carrying me along. I feel like we should hang on to one another's belts like we did on field trips in elementary school. We stop again, corralled by ropes linked to posts. Past the barriers are rows of tables, each set up with PC computers along either side. You show your yellow sheet to a guard to get into the gaming area, to prove you have a match coming up.

The tournament begins without fanfare. There are no big announcements, and no sign of Cyrus Popp. We pass the time by watching the battles projected on big screens around the room.

"Look. It's them." Max nudges me and points at one of the screens. Two Leothrawl and two Kwill are making short work of their opponents. It's the same combo of fighters we'd taken on two days ago.

"We don't know it's the same team," I tell him.

"Noah, what are the odds of a different team having the same four characters?"

"One in two point five six million," Noah says.

"You did the math that fast in your head?" Max asks.

"Nah, I figured it out before, and I have a good memory," Noah said. He taps his temple.

The Kwill blast through the wall and take their opponents' base. There's a smattering of applause from the group watching the screens. The winning team is called the Sigh Borgs. Making fun of Cyrus fans, I guess? Why would they do that? Cyrus Popp is awesome.

"That was epic," a curly haired guy says. He's about fifteen and wearing a polo shirt and crisp navy shorts, which makes him the best-dressed person in the tournament.

"They got lucky. They don't even have a balanced team," another guy comments. He has long dark bangs hanging in his face.

"Nah, they know what they're doing," Noah tells him.

"It's like a trick chess opening," the guy in the polo shirt says. "You trick your opponent into thinking you're a noob and get him into fool's mate."

I don't play chess, really, but I know about the fool's mate. Noah showed me how you can win in a few moves if your opponent is overconfident.

"Hey, I think I've seen you at chess tournaments," Noah says.

"Yeah, I've seen you too." They trade palm slaps.

"Anyway, they're definitely the team to beat," the long-haired guy says.

"We did beat them!" Zach chimes in.

"Sure you did."

"We did!" Zach insists. And he might be right. What with the odds Noah gave us. The same unlikely four characters, and the same high-speed fighting style. I scan the tables, trying to figure out which real-world faces belong to those lions and porcupines.

Max tugs on my arm.

"Come on, it's time!"

We weave our way through the crowd, show our yellow papers to the guards, and head down the long, tight space between two tables. Our first opponents are sitting across from us.

"No. Way." Max sits down with a thud.

"Way." Tori smiles at us. Three girls I don't know are with her.

"Madison, right?" Noah asks one. "You go to my church."

She nods, but her face is tough.

"Better get seated," Tori says. "The match is about to start."

We do. On each monitor you can see the time ticking down to the match. I click to begin and enter my login name and password. I remember I'm playing as Mustina today and feel a little lost for a moment, like people must do in those movies where they wake up as someone else. I see the other fighters appear on the screen in turn as Zach, Noah, and Max take their seats and log in. The match is already set. 4LMNTs vs. MadMachine.

3 . . . 2 . . . 1 . . . BATTLE!

There are a dozen arenas in *Smashtown Frenzy*, chosen at random. This one is called Rooftops. It's high in the city, the tops of buildings connected by narrow makeshift bridges. I *hate* this arena.

Pango crosses the first bridge, rounds a chimney, and storms toward enemy territory. He meets a Gurrilla on the second bridge and the two clash. It's almost like they're sumo wrestling—each trying to throw the other off the roof. I circle around to help and run into Burroughs, an aardvark assassin.

Mustina snaps and Burroughs retreats. Spike is right behind me. He puts his head down and charges. The aardvark jumps out of the way and slashes Spike's backside, taking lots of health. I glance up briefly and see Madison smiling evilly. She must be the assassin. I lunge after Burroughs, and we trade jabs and slashes until we're both dead. For thirty seconds we can only watch the battle, both of us waiting to respawn. Thirty seconds is a long time in a battle.

Pango wrenches free and does an effective roll attack, careening off the ape and going deeper into their territory. He smacks right into an Anthilla, a giant queen ant. She sends droves of ants out in front of her who do lots of damage. Anthilla is usually hard to fight, but she is not effective against Pango, who can gobble up the ants. I realize what good luck it is that Tori didn't know our team now has a Pango.

Meanwhile, our Pirrot has flapped and squawked in Gurrilla's face until the big ape finally stumbles off the ledge. We've got a three-on-two advantage, and it's time to go on attack. Spike takes a run at the wall while Pango stays in front of Anthilla, keeping her neutralized. Pirrot gives Spike a health boost, and he runs at the wall.

I finally respawn and race to the other side, arriving as Gurrilla respawns. Their assassin is also back. He's slashing at Pango. I jump into the fray, slashing and biting. Burroughs falls on his back, legs flailing. Pango sees an opportunity and rears up to get her with both front claws.

"Noooo!" I wail. In real life, I mean. In the game, Burroughs sees Pango's exposed stomach and slashes with his razor-sharp rear claws. The back roll is Burroughs's stealth move. A cheap, dirty stunt that Zach fell for. Pango is dead, which means Anthilla is free. She lets loose a cyclone of ants and—

Well, the girls are happier than us at the end of the match. Enough said.

"Good game!" Madison says brightly.

"Yeah," Max says.

"Sorry, bro," says Tori.

We start to leave, but Zach won't get up. He's hanging his head.

I tug on his shoulder. "Come on man, we have to clear out for the next team."

"I'm such a noob," he moans.

"No, you played really well, mostly. You fell for a trick move you'd never seen before. But now you know and you won't fall for it again."

"We lost because of me."

Which is true, but I see no reason to rub it in. As long as he knows.

"Come on, man. The next team is here."

Zach finally stands up and the four of us limp away.

"We lost the very first match," Noah says. He looks stunned.

"It's all my fault," says Zach, who is still moping.

Max looks at him, seeming to be wondering what a team leader does. He finally pats Zach's shoulder. "Look, it's double-elimination in the first round. We can't lose again, that's all."

CHAPTER 4

We have twenty minutes until our next match, enough time to take a bathroom break, drink some water, and head back to the hall. As we do, I hear a burst of applause and wonder if Cyrus Popp has finally made an appearance, but no. It's the Sigh Borgs trampling another team.

"They're so much fun to watch," I hear a kid say. "Breaking all the rules and getting away with it."

"They've won twice and are in the next round," Max observes. "Must be nice."

Fortunately our second match is easier. The other team must have signed up on a lark, because they aren't good. We take down their wall and seize the base without much trouble.

"What's your favorite kind of tree?" Zach asks after our opponents take off their headphones.

"Huh?" They look up in confusion.

"Elm? Oak?"

"I don't know," one of them says.

"Mine is VICK-TREE!" Zach whaps the table.

"Dude, don't act like a noob," Max says to Zach as we head back to the front of the hall for our next assignment.

"Would noobs lose?" Zach asks.

"Trash talk is for noobs," says Noah. "At least against bad teams."

I don't join in. I'm wondering how good we are. I know we're good with Tori, but without her . . . I'm not sure. We're only one and one today, and one team was terrible. I wish I had the confidence back that I had this morning.

Several teams have now won their first two matches and advanced to the next round, including MadMachine. Kids celebrate right in front us, hugging and dabbing and talking about where to get lunch before the second round. The camaraderie and cheer are still coursing through the crowd, but now I feel I'm on the outside looking in.

"The bright side," Noah says, "is that we're now playing other losers."

"We're not *losers*," Max says.

"I mean, literally. As in, they have lost a match," Noah explains. "We're likely to have more matches like the last one because the good teams have advanced. Except us, obv."

"Obv," Max agrees.

The third match is around noon. The other guys come at us fast and furious, three of them assassins, probably trying to duplicate the success of the Sigh Borgs. They do have one tank, but it hangs back, protecting the fortress wall, which makes the assassins easy to pick off. When we get through them it's four-on-one. I feel almost sorry for the guys as they mutter "good game" and slink away.

"They took a gamble and lost," Noah says. "We played it safe and won."

"I'd rather win ugly than lose pretty," Max says. "Come on. Let's grab lunch. I hear there are food trucks parked outside."

"Any that serve olive sandwiches?" I ask him.

"What? That sounds gross."

"You sound gross." I'm always ready with a grade-school comeback.

We find a Franky's Truck on Nicollet Avenue, and all of us fork over allowance money for hot dogs and chips. The day has gotten warm and balmy. It feels good after the over-air-conditioned convention center, but soon I feel hot and tired. There are no available benches so we park our behinds on a low retaining wall.

"Hey, are you guys in the tournament?" a *very* familiar voice asks: low, with a light southern accent. I look up. The man is a silhouette against the bright sunlight, but I see the long bill of his cap and know it's him. Cyrus Popp. Streamcast star. Tournament MC. Idol to millions of kids. He's got a couple women with him, one carrying a camera and one a smaller bag. His *entourage*, I think they're called.

I'm so excited I might stroke out, as he would say. I'm suddenly unable to speak. I glance over and see Zach is as freaked as I am, and Max is trying to find his tongue.

"Yep," Noah says casually. He's not into Streamcast. It's possible he doesn't even recognize Cyrus.

"We're the 4LMNTs," Max says at last, pronouncing it "four elements," because that's how we say it. "Numeral four, capital L—"

"Do you want to be in a video?" Cyrus interrupts.

"Yes!" Zach and I shout at the same time. We've been watching his recaps of tournaments in other cities. He always features a few random kids at the beginning. I can't believe we got picked out of the mob.

"Great," he says. "So how're the dogs? I like 'em Carolina style myself."

"We can do that!" the guy from the truck shouts. Cyrus walks over, explains about his Streamcast channel, and asks if he wants to be in the video. The food truck guy looks skeptical, but nods.

"OK, let's go," says Cyrus. The woman with the smaller bag powders his face a little, then comes over to us. "To take the shine off you, in the bright light," she explains and dabs at us all. So, for the first time in my life, I'm wearing makeup. Meanwhile, Cyrus has started recording his video over by the truck.

"Cyrus Popp here, coming to you from downtown Minneapolis, the eighth stop on our coast-to-coast *Smashtown Frenzy* tournament tour, where it is hotter than a hundred-dollar car. And if you know me, you know what I love most after gaming and making videos is a perfectly made hot dog. I'm told these are the best in town." He points with his thumb at the food truck behind him. The bearded guy in the window waves.

Cyrus turns his head and asks for two Carolina-style dogs, explaining that they're made with a special kind of wiener called a hot link. "That's super important," he says. "And topped with chili, mustard, onions, and coleslaw, *in that order.*" The food truck guy gives a thumbs-up to the camera while Cyrus tucks a twenty-dollar bill in the tip cup.

"While we're waiting, let's talk to some Cyborgs!" he says. And then we're on camera. The four of us wave and shout "Woot!" because we don't know what else to do. Cyrus and the camerawoman move closer, zeroing in on Noah, probably because he's the only one so far who's not starstruck and tongue-tied.

"How are you doing in the tournament so far?" Cyrus asks him.

"Good. Not great. But we're still in it."

"In it to win it!" Zach blurts out. The woman does a quick swivel with the camera to show his face, then back to Cyrus.

"And you're having fun!" It isn't exactly a question. More like stage directions.

"Loads," Noah says.

"Tremendous," Max adds.

"I'm having more fun than a tornado in a trailer park," I say, using one of Cyrus's own expressions, trying to mimic his accent. He points at me and laughs.

"He does me better than me!" he says to the camera before turning back to us.

"And how excited are you for the second round?" I know the cue. So do Zach and Max.

"We're so excited we're stroking out!" we say in unison, Noah joining in halfway through. We all do the face-boil bit with blinks and darting tongues until Cyrus waves at us to stop, then gives us a thumbs-up sign.

"Well, now it's time for the big test of the Minneapolis hot-dog game." Cyrus goes back to the truck and takes the paper tray, first making a big deal about crumbling potato chips on both, then takes a huge, messy bite of one. He holds his thumb out sideways and starts wiggling it, like the needle on a meter. He does that when he reviews games. It's called the Cyr-O-Meter. He finally swallows and the thumb goes straight up.

"This is a great hot dog!" he says. "If Minneapolis can smash noobs as well as they make wieners, it's going to be an amazing couple days!" He turns back to the truck. "You better be ready to sell a lot of hot dogs tomorrow." He leans in and whispers loud enough for the camera's mic to pick up his voice. "I'm kind of a big deal." The woman with the camera stops recording.

"Thanks," the hot-dog vendor says amiably as Cyrus and his team walk back toward the convention center.

"I can't believe that happened," Zach says.

"Me neither," I agree.

"Who *was* that guy?" the hot-dog vendor asks us.

• • •

Meeting Cyrus gives us a surge of confidence. We breeze through the next couple rounds. I barely notice who we're playing, neither the fighter characters nor the humans behind them. I storm in with my badger fighter and bite and claw my way through the enemies. Pango is my shield, and Spike comes up behind us to ram the wall. Pirrot circles overhead healthing everybody up, while Max barks orders over our headsets.

We are good after all! It's a huge relief.

By midafternoon they've rolled away some of the tables and set up rows of chairs so kids can watch matches on the big screen. They don't need as many tables because the competition has dwindled. We don't want to get psyched out, so we wander around the convention center instead of watching matches.

When we return, we see MadMachine leaving the gaming area. They look dejected.

"The Sigh Borgs got us," Tori explains.

"Darn. I wanted a rematch," Max says.

"Glad you guys are still in it," she says, and maybe she means it.

"In it to win it," he says.

There's a surge of excitement as people rush to the stage. Cyrus has appeared!

"Hello, Cyborgs!" The crowd shouts back a hello to him. "It is the end of day one in Minneapolis, and we have gone from more than five hundred teams to thirty-six. But only thirty-two will be back to play tomorrow. Thirty slots have already been taken. The last two spots are going to be determined right now, and we'll be showing the matches live on my Streamcast channel!" The crowd cheers.

"First up. I'm told these four are the team to beat in this tournament. The SIGH BORGS!"

Two Asian girls, carbon copies of each other, go up the

steps to the stage, followed by two light-haired boys. I blink. It's like seeing double.

"Two sets of twins," Max says. "Just like in the game."

"So," Cyrus says to one of the girls. "Sigh Borgs. Spelled S-I-G-H. That sounds like a bit of a rip on my fans."

The girl shrugs.

"Just a little joke," her twin sister says. I mean, it's got to be her twin, unless it's her clone.

"Are you feeling good about the next round?"

The first girl nods.

"We're in it to win it!" says her sister.

"Good luck!" Cyrus says. "And our next team is . . . the 4LMNTS!" He says it right, which is cool. He remembered!

We head up the steps single file, Max in the lead.

"Hey, it's my buddies from the hot-dog truck!" Cyrus tips his mic at Max. "How are you feeling about the next round?"

Max's face is frozen in fright.

"Do you like your chances?" Cyrus looks to Noah, who says nothing. Suddenly even *he* is starstruck. Cyrus looks at me.

I'm about to say, "We're in it to win it!" But as soon as I open my mouth, I remember the girl from the Sigh Borgs said the same thing, and Zach said it in the video Cyrus shot earlier. I need to come up with something else, but I'm not a freestyle rapper able to make up rhymes on the spot.

"What's your favorite kind of tree?" I ask him.

"Uh . . . maybe a pine tree," he says quickly.

"Ours is VICK-TREE!" I shout, stealing Zach's lame joke.

"Oh. Good for you." Cyrus pulls the mic away.

The crowd groans and mutters.

"What was that?" Noah asks me as we take our seats.

"I panicked," I admit.

The Sigh Borgs look at us almost with pity. They put on their headphones and get ready to play.

"Psst. Be Trunky," Noah tells me through the mic after I get my own headset on.

"We'll have two tanks?"

"Three actually. Max is going to be Ursalot, a big mama bear. If they want to go double damage, we'll counter with triple protection. But I'll still be Spike."

"*Three* tanks and a cannon." It's the craziest thing I've ever heard.

"A trick chess opening needs a good countermove," he tells me. "They want a quick match? So we'll grind it to a halt."

"Fine. What have we got to lose?"

"The match. The tournament. Our registration fees."

"Right." I log in and switch to Trunkzilla. It's like putting on a pair of sneakers after wearing dress shoes all day. So much more comfortable. I feel like I could jump over a building.

3 . . . 2 . . . 1 . . . BATTLE!

Trunkzilla plants his elephant feet in front of our fortress wall. On his left is Pango, and on his right is Ursalot. The Leothrawl speed down to slash and bite at us, and the Kwill roll up behind them.

We each get off one of our minor attacks: Stomp! Smack! Maul! The Leothrawl back away, letting their health creep up a bit. The Kwill roll in and detonate, blasting us and the wall.

Ursalot is the first to go, but the porcupines also deal damage to each other. They step back and the Leothrawl return.

Meanwhile, Spike sneaks his way down the side lane. Not a single defender is there to stop him. He starts to hammer their wall.

It's a simple race against time. Their assassins throw themselves at us, slashing and biting. One is too slow to retreat and vanishes from the screen.

The Kwill take another shot, shattering our wall and taking Pango out of the match, but both disappear.

There's a standoff with Trunky and Leothrawl, both with the slightest bars of health. The base is exposed behind my fighter.

The lion sprints past me, taking me by surprise. He lunges at the base.

YOU WIN.

The words splash across the screen. I'm confused. The Leothrawl landed on our base, but it hasn't turned red. And the message says we won?

I finally get it. Spike landed on their base a split second ahead of the Leothrawl.

There's a smattering of cheers and applause mixed up with some groans. The Sigh Borgs have picked up a lot of fans throughout the day.

"Good game," I tell the two sets of twins after we take off our headphones. I notice the girls are kind of gorgeous.

"No rematch," Noah adds, remembering what they said after our online battle—assuming it really is the same team.

We make our way out of the room, trading dabs and high fives with a lot of gamers while others call us lucky. One is the curly haired boy in the polo shirt from earlier.

"You got away with one," he says.

But I know something he doesn't know: We've beaten the Sigh Borgs before.

"And we'll be back tomorrow for the second day in Minneapolis!" Cyrus says at the end. "I'm so excited—"

He does his usual bit. I don't play along this time—I'm too drained. Deliriously happy but also exhausted. Suddenly I just want to be sitting in a comfy chair with a cat on my lap, listening to a mystery novel with my friend Isaac.

• • •

I watch Cyrus's video when I get home. It's fun to see us featured at the hot-dog truck. It's not as much fun to see myself shout a bunch of blather on the stage. My voice is higher than I think it is. The vick-tree joke is terrible and sounds obnoxious.

But it's fun again to see Cyrus's commentary on that last match. I couldn't hear it when I was playing because of my headphones. Whenever he refers to the Sigh Borgs he actually *sighs*, then adds "Borgs," in this bored way that's really funny.

"This is crazy," he says when the Leothrawl come up against our tanks. "Unstoppable force versus immovable object." The Leothrawl go on attack and start to lose health. "I think their eyes are bigger than their stomachs," he says with a laugh. "But uh-oh, here come the Kwill. Boom goes the porcupine!"

When we win, he literally screams in excitement. "That

was closer than a hair on a hog!" Spike hits the base while the Leothrawl is midpounce. But there seems to me more boos than I remember. That makes me uneasy. I have never really done anything where people clap for me, like sports or acting in a play, but I've never been booed either.

"Lots of people booed us yesterday," I tell Dad the next morning as he backs out of the driveway. He's driving me downtown for the second day of the tournament.

"Oh yeah? How come?"

"We beat the team they were rooting for."

"I see. Well, you said it was a sport, so that's going to happen. Don't take it personally. Remember when we saw the Saint Paul Saints and you booed the team from Sioux Falls, even though you'd never heard of them before?"

"Yeah." He has a point. I'm not a huge baseball fan, but I got into it with the rest of the crowd.

"I bet you have some fans too?" he says.

"Sure. Maybe."

I notice Isaac's house as Dad turns onto the interstate and wonder how he's doing. I should have asked if he wanted to come today, I think. He liked the short video I showed him. Maybe he'd get swept up in the action. He'd see what a big deal this is.

There are already a lot of kids hanging around outside the convention center, enjoying the sunshine before they go into the cold building.

"I would stay and watch," Dad says, "but . . ."

"I know. You don't really care about video games."

"I was *going* to say, I have a job interview. I feel good about this one. It's managing the same kind of database I managed before."

"Oh. Wow. Good luck."

"And, of course, we care, kiddo. Your mother and I aren't into games, but we're proud of you for working so hard, and *we're* rooting for you. Never think otherwise."

"I know. And thanks."

"And about those guys booing you," he says.

"Yeah?"

"Winning is the best revenge."

• • •

Today's matches are in an auditorium on the first floor instead of the ballrooms. I check in and get ushered past the audience to a cordoned-off area in front of the theater-style seats. The gaming tables are on a stage with two big screens behind them for showing the action. I plop down next to Zach and Max. Noah joins us a moment later. The area slowly fills up. I notice the curly haired guy who called us lucky sitting a few seats away. He gives me a slight nod and turns back to his phone. I didn't know he was a contender.

"Good game yesterday," a tall girl tells us as she squeezes past.

"Thanks." I realize that the other teams are *all* older at this point. We seem to be the only middle-schoolers left in the tournament. That might explain some of the people rooting against us. They don't want to be shown up by some young

punks. And I made things worse when I blurted out that vick-
tree joke.

I calm myself down a bit. These guys don't hate us any
more than I hate the Sioux Falls Canaries. It was just part of
the game.

The seats outside the winners' area fill up too. I keep
swiveling back to look. Most of the kids who've been eliminated
have come back. But there are more people today than there
were yesterday, so a bunch of people must be coming to watch,
the same way they go to baseball games. We're not simply
playing anymore. We're *performing*.

I feel nervous about that, but it's also thrilling. I can't throw
or catch a ball, can't sing or act or do the splits. But all those
people will be watching me do something I *am* good at. It's an
amazing feeling. For the first time in my life, I'm *somebody*.

I wish again I'd invited Isaac too, so he could see what a big
deal this is.

"Hello, Cyborgs!" Cyrus's voice crackles over the PA.

The crowd cheers.

"We're about to get started with day two of the Minneapolis
Smashtown Frenzy tournament. We have gone from more than
five hundred teams to thirty-two. And in a few hours, we will
winnow that down to four teams who will go on to the national
tournament. But of course we will also play on and name a
tournament champion. Who will be the top dogs?" I swear
that he's glancing at us when he says *top dogs*, that he thinks
we're the new team to beat. Well, who am I to argue? He's a
professional gamer. He would know.

Cyrus explains that the next round of matches will be played two at a time, splashed across big screens on either side of the stage. He starts reading out the first set of matches, milking it for drama. I really want to be in the first set, but no such luck.

The matches begin. My eyes drift back and forth between the two screens but barely register who is winning and losing. The matches end. Eight players return happily to our area, eight walk dejectedly to the audience. The next round begins. And then another. A *Smashtown* battle is usually between five and ten minutes long, and the people running the tournament don't waste any time between matches.

We don't play until the eighth and final pair, and Cyrus calls our name second. "4LMNTs!" he yells, and once again a mix of boos and jeers interrupt the polite cheering.

"Haters gonna hate," Zach says.

"Winning is the best revenge," I tell them, repeating my dad's words.

CHAPTER 5

The match is against the ReptylBois, four guys you'd expect to see in a skate park. They're all wearing baggy shorts, Vans shoes, and aloof expressions. We trade respectful nods before the match begins.

3 . . . 2 . . . 1 . . . BATTLE!

The arena is Travesty Park, which looks like a vacant lot overrun with weeds and vines. It has lots of places to hide, all of them flammable. Which is bad for us because they have a Fumungus, a salamander-like cannon that coughs fire. He is already igniting the jungle, which flames out quickly but smolders and smokes.

Their tank, Tortuga, a gigantic tortoise, marches through the wreckage. He's slow and doesn't have any good offensive moves, but he's big and resilient; the tankiest of the tanks.

We've been playing with our default characters all day— Max as Pirrot the parrot, Noah as Spike the rhino, Zach as Pango the pangolin, and me as Mustina the badger. I wish we'd noticed the ReptylBois and known about the Fumungus. We could have countered with something that can put out fires.

"Don't waste moves on the turtle," Max says. "Take out the lizard."

"Salamanders aren't lizards," Noah tells him.

"I don't care. Kill it."

He means for *me* to kill it, but I don't want to get trapped in a burning clump of weeds. I scamper past the Fumungus and circle around the Tortuga, meaning to use the tank as my shield. But I run into Krawk, as in crocodile, the biggest and least squishy assassin there is. He is big and slow and can't turn around in tight spots, which explains the ReptylBois' strategy: Burn and trample a path for Krawk.

Now I'm stuck between two enemies: Fumungus behind me and Krawk in front. I try to escape to the side, but a burst of fire from Fumungus ignites my escape path. It's hard to ignore the noise of excitement from the audience. They are rooting for me to die. To make matters worse, Dracomiga appears. A giant dragonfly, Dracomiga gives its teammates an attack boost when it hums. It is humming now.

I try my badger's stealth move to get behind Krawk, but he's too big to get around. I avoid a chomp, but get swiped by his tail and take extra damage from the Dracomiga boost. I dodge another swipe and get backed up against the smoldering jungle. Max's Pirrot flies overhead to restore my health, but this only stalls my impending doom. The audience is doing a steady clap, clap, clap, like they do in a baseball game when the opponents are down to their last out.

It's not personal, I remind myself. *And winning is the best revenge.* When the humming stops, I go all out on the Krawk's tail, biting and slashing, dodging as he lunges around, taking advantage of how lousy he is at turning in tight circles. Pirrot helps, diving down to stab at his eyes and get in his face.

"Time to make you into alligator shoes!" I take a swipe at the Krawk's face. I add another stealth move to avoid the tail, get in some final licks, and watch him flicker and fade.

I hear Zach snickering over my headset, and Noah muttering, "It's a crocodile, not an alligator."

The Fumungus has been holding back, not wanting to hurt the Krawk, but now he's got only me in his path so he hurries forward with a jet of fire. I avoid the jet but find myself trapped on every side. Pango rolls past the salamander and through the smoldering jungle, taking damage to clear me a path. I escape to the side lane.

I'm aware of the noise behind me—the crowd shouting and hooting, people stomping their feet and clapping. I've been so focused on the game I was shutting it all out.

"Attack or defend?" I ask over the mic. We have only a moment to decide, and we have to all decide the same thing.

"Attack!" Max says even as I ask.

So we do, leaving the Fumungus and Tortuga to scorch and trample their way to our fortress wall. Their only defense is the dragonfly, who dives feebly at us, but that's not its role.

We realize too late we've stranded Spike behind the enemies and the fire. So Pango and Mustina take on the fortress, and neither of us is particularly good at bringing down a wall. I flail at it, biting and clawing, while Pango executes a roll and smacks into it, which is slightly more effective. I hear voices shouting louder and louder in unison.

Bring it down! Bring it down!

I don't know if they're cheering for us or the other team. Our own wall is on fire and about to fall. But theirs is also close to crumbling.

Spike charges at the Fumungus, sacrificing himself to deal as much damage as possible. Pirrot circles back to health him up, but it's too late. The rhino is dead. The parrot squawks and dive-bombs the salamander, trying to delay the final blast of fire. The fat tortoise lumbers into the way.

Pango takes one last roll at their wall, jarring a few bricks lose as he smacks into it. Their Krawk respawns, leaping out with a big chomp that gets Pango on the tail and takes the last of his health. The crowd is going nuts now. Mustina meets Krawk head on, but the reptile has full health and the badger doesn't. He makes short work of her. I hear a roar behind me. People whooping and stomping. It's four against one, and the one fighter we have left is a bird. But there's a hole in the ReptylBois' fortress wall. Max sees it, sails over it with Pirrot, and hits their base a mere second before our own wall comes down.

You win splashes across our screens.

The crowd falls dead silent. It's like the air has been sucked out of the room. It was four against one . . . a full-strength team against a *parrot*, and somehow . . . We won.

Or maybe, if I'm being honest, *Max* won.

"Are you kidding me?" Cyrus shouts. "Are you kidding me? These kids are luckier than a butcher's hound dog!"

I glance back and see people with their hands on their heads, jaws slack.

"Good game," I tell our opponents. They look stunned. One of them is blinking back tears, way out of character for cool guys.

"Yeah," he says glumly. "Good game."

• • •

The next few matches are a blur. We face Burroughs and Leothrawl again, and beat them again. We survive Squunk's stink bombs, Kwill's hurling spines, Raptora's gales of wind, and Zigzap the eel's electric field. We even take on Trunkzilla. It's hard for me to unleash Mustina's fury on a character I love so much. But we eke out a victory there after their Trunkzilla is fried by their own Zigzap, leaving the lane clear for us to storm their fortress. There's some applause, but also the usual groans and boos.

"You've got to love these kids," Cyrus says, but not everyone agrees.

"Congrats," one of our opponents tells us. I remember her from the morning. She's one of the few players in the winners' circle who's been nice to us. The tall girl. "You made the finals."

"Huh?" I've been taking one match at a time and lost track. I thought there was one more after this. I glance down to the winners' area and see she's right. It was packed this morning, but now there are only a few people scattered around. We're in the top four, which means we get to advance to Chicago, no matter what happens.

I'm at peace with the haters now. We proved that we were good.

"*I'll* be rooting for you," she says.

"Thanks!" At least somebody is, besides my parents.

The final three matches to determine the city champs will be staged one at a time, and we're on first. Our opponents are four girls in matching yellow T-shirts, each with Mustina's shape emblazoned across it in black. Their team name is *Diggory*.

"Harry Potter fans," Noah theorizes in a whisper. "They think they're Hufflepuffs."

"Aren't Hufflepuffs the nerds?" Zach asks.

"Dude, we're at a gaming tournament," Max interjects. "It might as well be a Hufflepuff convention."

Zach snickers.

Diggory may go with the badger as their symbol, but once we jump into the game we see they aren't playing with Mustina. Their assassin is Ringo. Nobody agrees on what he's supposed to be: a lemur, a raccoon, a red panda? They also have Squunk the stink-bomber for a cannon and Chiron the bat for support. Their tank is Cleo, a gigantic armored beetle. It's like they deliberately went with the least popular fighter in every category. Which is a total Hufflepuff move, I think. And not a bad strategy because we're not used to playing against these characters. For example, I forget that Ringo flings mud—I sure hope it's mud—until he spatters us and deals damage. And I haven't exactly forgotten that Chiron can plunge the arena into darkness, but I've forgotten how frustrating it is to stumble about in the dark.

We play clumsily, dragging out a battle in the middle of the map. Max sacrifices Pirrot to take out the bat. Mustina takes some damage to get close to Ringo, because he's less effective in close combat. She takes him out, straggles away, and is done in by their skunk's stink bomb.

Now it's a two-on-two match, tanks and cannons. Once again, I'm glad that Noah has refused to give up Spike. He's an early character to unlock and does less damage against enemies, but he's a great cannon for taking down an opponent's fortress. Squunk is one of the most damaging cannons to enemies, but it takes a long time to bring down a wall with stink bombs.

"The objective of the game is to *take the opponents' base,*" Noah says, and usually follows it up with a chess analogy.

Their wall crumbles and Spike storms in for another win.

"Great game," Noah says to the Hufflepuffs as we slap hands, and he means it. I wish they could have stayed in it, since they seem pretty cool.

The four of us are now alone in the winners' area while the other semifinal is played. I try to get interested in the match, thinking about which of the teams we want to play and how we would play them, but I have trouble concentrating. I'm too stressed out thinking about the next match.

Only Zach is relaxed, watching the ongoing match with a slightly open mouth, smiling and laughing.

"Ooooh!" he says, wincing, as one team's Isborg—a polar bear—is leveled by the other team's Leothrawl. Of course Zach can take it all in stride. He's only on the team because of a sudden vacancy, and now he's in the finals. But when the Leothrawl takes a face full of ink from the first team's Kathulopter, a flying squid, I join in his cheer. I don't know why we're rooting for the polar bear and the squid, but it doesn't matter.

The team with the polar bear and squid takes control of the match, but doesn't end it. They seem to be playing for time, toying with the opposition. They give the Leothrawl time to respawn so they can fight him again.

"Who are these guys?" Max asks. "I haven't noticed them." The team is actually two guys and two girls.

"They're called KidsfromSLP," Noah tells him. SLP is short for Saint Louis Park, one of the inner-ring suburbs of Minneapolis. "They play with different characters every time, which is probably why you don't remember them."

"That's kind of weird," Zach says, and I agree. Most players get comfortable with one character. Swapping around is either a noob mistake or showing off. Since this team is in the finals, it's not a noob mistake.

"I bet they play with different characters so they can fly under the radar," Noah says.

"And chose a boring name for the same reason," Max offers.

"There's no target on their back," I say. Which makes them smarter than us and the Sigh Borgs. Maybe they've been the team to beat all along?

The Kids finally claim their opponents' base and win the match. Cyrus walks across the stage toward them. One of them stands up to meet him. It's the well-dressed, curly haired boy.

The one who was rooting for the Sigh Borgs and says we got lucky. Cyrus shakes his hand and turns to the crowd.

"We are now down to the final match. I'm so excited—" We all know the bit. The crowd strokes out along with him.

But we're too busy tromping up onto the stage one last time to join in. The older kids seem so cool and confident. I feel a little bit doomed.

Cyrus calls the names of both teams. The crowd cheers for both, but it sounds like they cheer a lot louder for the KidsfromSLP.

We sit down and log in.

The screen behind us fills with the split screen that appears before a match. On the top is Mustina, Pango, Spike, and Pirrot. On the bottom, a second Pango appears, Caprina the girl ram, Honeypie the bee, and Vile the snake. They're playing with the starters—the level-zero fighters total beginners choose from. In theory, the characters are all equal, strengths balanced out by weaknesses, but these are the fighters everybody knows best, which makes them easier to defeat. The KidsfromSLP don't want to show off. They want to show us up.

Cyrus Popp shouts along with the text on the screen, and the crowd joins in.

"Three . . . two . . . one . . . Battle!" The chorus reaches a crescendo that is nearly deafening. And the match is underway.

The arena is Grimm's Fallow, a broad, muddy expanse without shelter. It's a great arena for Trunkzilla, who can tread through the mud easily. It's not as good for Mustina. She has to worry about getting stuck in the ooze. I steer her up the middle lane, where she's met by Vile. The two assassins dance, lunging and dodging, feinting and retreating, Mustina being careful to stay on the path.

Our Pango avoids the path, rolling through the mud to get into their territory. Spike follows; he's good in the mud. Vile breaks away to attack them, leaving me uncovered. I glance up and see their Caprina heading down a side lane, unguarded, into our territory. I'm free to go on defense, but a sudden warning sounds in my head. It's the voice of Ross Cooper. Or rather, the narrator of the Ross Cooper audiobooks.

Don't run. That's what they expect.

So I chase Vile, pouncing on the snake's tail and pulling him into a wrestling match while Spike runs at their wall. The snake breaks free and tries to slither away, but Pango gets in his way. Spike hits the wall, backs up, and runs again. Honeypie drops a load of sticky goo to slow him down. I take another lunge at the snake as he tries to get away, staying on his tail like a bratty little brother.

Caprina puts her horns down and hurls herself at our fortress. When it comes to flat-out wall-crushing, she might be the strongest there is. I do the math and timing in my head. Caprina needs four or five punches on the wall, Spike needs maybe six. He had a head start, but the honey will slow him down, so . . .

We're doomed. There's no way around it.

Pirrot flutters in Caprina's face, but she tosses him off with her horns.

I keep harassing the snake. Even if we lose, I will kill this snake, I think. We will go down fighting.

Spike tries to muster up speed despite the honey and gives their wall another bang, less effective than the first one. Pango tries to help but the rolling move that gets him through mud doesn't work in honey.

Speaking of Pango, where is theirs? My heart sinks when I see he's across the field, throwing his own weight into our wall, helping Caprina. There's no way we'll win the race to the base. We are absolutely 100 percent doomed.

But I can still kill that snake. I pull off a feint attack and glance up to see the curly haired kid glaring at me. They're winning, but he can't stand the fact that he's losing a one-on-one battle to me.

The snake dies and disappears. Our wall crumbles, the base is exposed, but their tank and cannon hold back. All they have to do is step through the hole to win the match, but they don't. The auditorium buzzes. What's going on?

I glance up and see the curly haired boy with the slightest smirk on his face.

He notices me and winks. I get the message. He wants to fight me again. He wants revenge. He wants to show me up and make the audience roar. Their wall is still standing, and Spike is mired in honey, so he thinks they've got plenty of time. He'll respawn and come after me, kill me, *then* win the match.

The Ross Cooper voice sends me another message.

It's a game of cat and mouse. But the mouse has an advantage if he can think like a cat.

These guys played cat and mouse with the last team, and

73

they plan to do it again with us. But I know exactly what these cats are thinking.

"Pango, be our wall," I tell Zach. "I'll take out their cannon."

I spring down the center lane, veering around their Pango to slash at Caprina. The ram lowers her horns and charges. I leap out of the way but still take some damage. It is worth it. I've led her away from our base, and Pango steps in to protect it. Pirrot flashes her wings and restores some of my health.

The honey has worn off, and Honeypie has to wait a few seconds for her special move to recharge. It's a big few seconds for us. But the moment Spike is able to charge, Vile respawns and gets in the way.

I keep up the game with Caprina, letting her lunge at me again and again, zigging and zagging down around the patches of mud in the middle of the map. She doesn't even notice that I'm leading her back to her own wall, where I plant myself and let her charge. I hit escape to leave the match and tap Y to confirm.

The badger disappears. Caprina crashes into their wall with a wallop. The wall collapses. Honeypie makes a mad buzz toward our base, but she hasn't got a chance. Spike tramples past the snake and over the crumbling wall to take their base.

YOU WIN. The words zip across the screens on either side of me.

And once again the crowd is stunned into silence. Even Cyrus is at a loss for words.

CHAPTER 6

Gamers swarm around the front of the convention center after the tournament. I hide behind a pillar until I see Dad's dark green Hyundai, way back in the slow-moving line of parents getting their kids. I hurry over and climb into the car, brushing past a couple kids who recognize me, but don't have a chance to say anything before I slam the car door.

"You all right?" Dad asks.

"Yep. We won first place." I show him the trophy, a brass-colored replica of a game controller mounted on a solid base. It's the first actual trophy I've ever gotten, and I'm embarrassed to realize how much this piece of plastic and fake wood means to me.

"No kidding? Lucas, that's incredible!" He sees an opening in the next lane and cranks his wheel to get into it. "I mean, we knew you could do it. But, you know. There were a lot of kids in the tournament. Nice trophy, kiddo."

"There's a check too. It'll pay for our trip to Chicago." Mom and Dad had been worrying about it, looking at the cheapest hotels in Chicago.

"That's great! So how come you look so glum?"

"Tired, I guess. It was a long day." *Forget anyone who says e-sports aren't real sports,* I think. I'm as tired as any guy coming out of an overtime football game.

"I'll bet." He wends his way through downtown, not pumping me for any more info. Maybe because he can tell I'm not up to it. Maybe because he needs to concentrate on rush-hour traffic. As we take the exit off the interstate from downtown I have an idea.

"Dad, can we go see Isaac?"

"Sure."

"Take the first left past the on-ramp," I remind him.

He takes the right turn and pulls over to the curb near Isaac's house. I grab the trophy as I get out of the car. Dad knocks on Isaac's door. There's no answer.

"Maybe he's not home?" he suggests.

"It always takes him a while."

Dad knocks again. We hear stumbling around inside, and the door swings open.

"Well, hello," Isaac says. His words are slurred. "Kind of late for you?"

"Yeah, we were passing by, and I thought I'd drop in and do the cat boxes because we're leaving for a few days. This is my dad." They've met before, but only for a few minutes.

"Nick Sabbatini," Dad reminds him, offering a hand. Isaac reaches for it awkwardly and misses. Dad takes Isaac's hand and gives it a pump.

"Come in, come in." Isaac waves us in. "Did you win your

Pac-Man tournament?" he asks me. I'm about to correct him but see from the lopsided smile on his face that he's trolling me a little.

"First place." I show him the trophy. He acts as if he's going to take the trophy, but changes his mind, dropping his hand.

"Wonderful. I knew you could do it."

"Ross Cooper actually helped," I tell him, remembering the line that proved crucial in the final match.

Isaac plops down heavily into his chair. "I had to return that one to the library. But Ross Cooper got away by getting those men to throw him overboard and he swam to shore." He muddles the words; they come out: "He sham to swore."

"I knew he would," I tell him as I head downstairs to scoop the cat boxes. Petey comes down and gives me a look.

"I'll wait, buddy," I tell him. "Take your time." I stand aside but he doesn't use the box. He gives me a look like something is wrong. "Fine." I go back to scooping. I wash my hands in the laundry sink and head back up.

". . . never did care much for fireworks," Isaac is saying, or trying to say, but he gets lost in the word "fireworks." Dad must have asked Isaac how he was spending the Fourth of July.

"Is he all right?" Dad whispers.

"I don't know," I whisper back.

Isaac is making perfect sense. He remembers that I had the tournament today. He remembers exactly where I left off in the middle of an audiobook. But he can't seem to talk clearly. I remember the look Petey gave me in the basement. It was like he was trying to tell me something. Maybe that Isaac needed help.

"We should call somebody," he says, not whispering anymore.

I grab my phone and call 911. Dad starts to say something, but I hold up my hand. The operator is on. She asks if it's a life-or-death situation. I tell her I'm not sure.

"I'm with an old man and I think he's having a seizure or something," I tell her. I explain about the slurred speech and the stumbling. "Ask him to smile and tell me if his face droops," the operator says.

"Can you smile?" I ask Isaac. He tries. It's the same lopsided smile he made when he joked about the *Pac-Man* tournament

"Yeah, it's drooping," I tell her. "It kind of always does, but it looks worse than usual."

"Ask him to hold both arms out for ten seconds."

I repeat the instructions. Isaac gets his arms out, but one drifts down again. I remember how he'd reached for the trophy and failed. And he had trouble shaking dad's hand.

"He can't do it," I tell the operator.

"There's a very good chance your friend has had a stroke," she says, her voice now full of urgency. "We'll send an ambulance." I give her the address and stay on the line until she tells me the ambulance is on its way.

"She says it might be . . . a stroke," I tell Dad. My voice cracks. I take a deep, shuddering breath. I don't even know what a stroke is, but I know it's serious.

Isaac leans in, a frightened look on his face. "What's that? Am I going to be all right?"

• • •

The EMTs are there in about five minutes. They help Isaac into the back and the ambulance speeds away, siren wailing. I find a key in the kitchen, but it's to the kitchen door, so we lock the front from the inside and leave through the back. Dad calls the Senior Sitting place because we don't know who else to call or how to get a hold of them. Fortunately somebody is still there and answers. She tells us she'll notify Isaac's emergency contacts.

"We might not be able to go to the cabin," I realize on the way home. We're supposed to leave the next day. "Somebody has to take care of his cats."

"Oh, Lucas," Dad says. I think he means, *Oh, Lucas, don't use this to try to get out of the family trip.* He turns into the parking lot of a grocery store about halfway home, like he suddenly remembers we need eggs and milk. But he sits there a moment, and I realize he's shaking.

"My God, Lucas. What if we hadn't dropped in on him?" His voice is hoarse.

"It's all right," I tell him. "We did drop in on him."

"I'm so proud of you." He runs a hand through his thinning hair. "You were really levelheaded and calm in there."

"Well, you raised me, so be proud of both of us."

He laughs, takes another minute to collect himself, and drives home.

"Well?" Mom says as we walk into the kitchen. She's preparing to do something with a can of chickpeas. "How did it go?"

How did what go? I wonder. I've completely forgotten about the tournament. It seems so long ago and far away. I even left my trophy at Isaac's house. Dad explains what happened to Isaac in a low voice. Mom gasps and covers her mouth with one hand.

"Lucas, are you OK?"

"Sure. I will be." I tromp upstairs to my room. My eyes are hot and my whole body hurts. For once I don't even want to get online. I take off my shoes, lie down on my bed, and close my eyes. I see Isaac's fearful look.

"Am I going to be all right?" he asked. *Is he?*

I remember Petey's imploring look down in the basement. I have a sudden desire to cycle there as fast as I can, to find Petey and tell him I'm sorry it took us so long.

"Hey, kiddo." Dad pushes the door open. I blink in confusion, see the red numbers on the clock. It's 7:46. I must have drifted off to sleep. "There's dinner downstairs. We're keeping it warm for you. Chickpea hash and yellow rice. It's better than it sounds!"

"All right. I'll be down in a second."

I grab my phone and look at my feed. I subscribe to all kinds of gaming channels, and there are a lot of updates about the tournament.

Minneapolis Upstarts Rage Quit to Victory

Epic Fail or Epic Luck? Watch This Incredible Smashtown Meltdown

Cyrus Popp Recaps Day 2 in Minneapolis

I click that one, fast forwarding through some of it until the final match.

"What are the KidsfromSLP doing?" Cyrus hollers when

our own wall comes down and our opponents don't seize the base. "This is crazy," he says when we take theirs a moment later. "These 4LMNTs are luckier than raccoons during a garbageman strike!"

It's pretty cool to see it again, but I also notice the comments popping up below the video.

The whole match is fixed.

Yeah, that other team didn't even throw the game convincingly.

So some people think the match is fixed, and Cyrus thinks we're lucky. It's true that the KidsfromSLP could have won that match, but they tried to play cat and mouse with us and got out-catted.

I put down the phone and head downstairs. Right now, Streamcast is even less appetizing than chickpea hash.

• • •

Early the next morning I bicycle to Isaac's. It's not too warm yet, but I can tell from the dampness in the air that it will be. I lock my bike to a laundry pole in the backyard and let myself in the kitchen door using the key Dad and I took. I feel like an intruder. The cats are pacing and meowing. I wash out their food bowls and refill them. Petey yowls from the counter the entire time. The black one is Sam, Isaac's usual lap cat, and he looks especially confused and upset.

"He'll be back soon," I tell him and hope it's true.

It doesn't feel like I've done enough, so I wash the rest of the dishes, three loads worth, dry them with a clean towel I find in a drawer, and stack them on the counter. I head into the living room and start straightening books. That's a lost cause. There are too many of them and no place to put them. I wonder why Isaac keeps so many books that he's probably already read, and won't read again since his eyes are so bad.

One catches my eye. *She's on the Case.* A lot of Isaac's books have lurid covers. This one doesn't. Instead of the tough-looking white man staring out at the reader and the scantily clad woman in the background, this one has a serious-looking black woman in a business suit. Instead of a gun, she has a briefcase.

The author's name is Isaac Biddle . . . ? I flip it over and read the back. There's no author photo but the bio says Isaac Biddle lives in Minneapolis and this is his first book. It must be him!

I sit down in my usual chair and start reading. Petey plants himself in my lap. Enough light spills through the slightly open curtains that I don't need to turn on a light.

The woman on the cover is named Billie Ruth. She's a public defender and her newest client shows up in a lavender leisure suit, talking fast and coming across super guilty. I get the feeling the client is going to be dead by the end of chapter one, and Billie will spend the rest of the book sleuthing out who killed him.

I hear footsteps on the porch, then the rattling of the doorknob. I freeze. Is somebody breaking in? Or is Isaac home?

The door swings open, and I see the silhouette of a huge person against the bright morning light. I scream. The shadow screams back. Petey leaps in fright and scampers away.

"Oh!" says a woman. She steps in, carrying a little suitcase with wheels, which she sets down. "You must be the boy," she says. "Why are you sitting in the dark like a burglar?" She pulls the curtain all the way open, filling the room with light. "You scared the life out of me."

I don't admit that she did the same to me. "I came to feed the cats and I guess I got used to the dark. My name is Lucas."

"I'm Yolanda. Isaac told me about you."

"You're the one who brings him books on tape," I remember.

"I bring him library books. Groceries. Take him to the doctor. Do his laundry. It's like being a mother to an eighty-year-old teenager!" Her voice is more affectionate than cross.

"He is pretty old," I offer. "Don't old people usually need help with things?"

"Ha. He was the same way forty years ago when I met him." She lets out a long sigh.

"How did you meet him?" I ask.

"I'm an old friend of the family," she says. "You know his mother, Margaret Ruth Biddle?"

The name *does* ring a bell, but I'm not sure why. I shrug.

"She was my mentor and friend for many years," Yolanda says. "There's nothing I wouldn't do for her. So before she left, when she asked me to take care of Isaac, I said I would. Mind you, I love Isaac like an uncle. Maybe more like a *nephew*, even though he's got twenty years on me. The man could never get his nose out of his books long enough to take care of himself."

"I like Isaac," I offer. "He's a good guy."

"Hmm-hmm." I'm not sure if she's agreeing with me or biting her tongue. "Well, he asked me to take care of the house and cats, so you're off the hook."

"Oh." I don't want to be off the hook. I like being here with the cats. "So is he going to be home soon?"

"In a few days, we hope," she says. "He needs to stay there for a few days, and then have around-the-clock observation for several months. He's at high risk for another stroke."

"OK." I don't know how to ask what I really want to know, which is if Isaac will still be . . . Isaac. She seems to guess by the look at my face.

"A stroke is very serious, especially for a man of Isaac's age."

I nod.

"We're going to have to find permanent care for him. And sort out his finances." She shakes her head sadly. "So. I'll be here until further notice. There's nobody else in Isaac's life right now."

"Except me," I remind her. "But uh . . . I won't be for a few days. My family is going to a cabin in the woods. But can you let me know if there's news?"

"I will," she says. "I have your home number."

I still have *She's on the Case*, which I want to keep reading. "Do you think he'd mind if I borrowed this book?"

"Of course not," she says. I wonder if that means Isaac won't know anyway. But she continues. "The doctor said you might have saved his life, and you definitely saved his brain. If he hadn't gotten help last night. Well . . . I think borrowing a book or two is the least you can ask for."

"Thanks." I am starting for the door when she surprises me by grabbing me and giving me a hug.

"You're a hero, Lucas," she says. "In case you didn't know."

CHAPTER 7

I spend most of the next week coated in sweat while mosquitoes feast on my blood. I venture out into the cold lake once or twice, feeling slimy lake-floor goo on my bare feet. I paddle a dinghy out into the middle of the lake once with Dad. But I don't feel a deep bond with nature, or whatever Mom and Dad were hoping. Nature is gross.

The closest thing to an adventure I have is wandering down paths in search of a cell phone signal, which I don't find, and getting a little bit lost before I find my way back.

One rainy afternoon we drive into "town," which is about four buildings on a gravel road. There's a post office, a general store, a bait and tackle shop, and a place that will mount your catch on a plaque. I wander into the bait shop and make an extraordinary find.

"I don't know, Lucas, it's kind of pricey," Dad says when I show him the long-billed fishing cap. It looks *exactly* like Cyrus Popp's. Same brand, same olive color. Same adult size too,

I discover when I put it on and it covers my eyes.

"This is a pretty cheap vacation," I remind him. "The cabin is free and we're making our own meals."

"True. But then we have a trip to Chicago."

"My prize money will pay for that!"

"It won't cover all our expenses," Dad says with a sigh. But the cashier rings up the hat and lets me keep it. I angle it back over my head with the bill in the air, the way Cyrus wears his sometimes, and feel very cool.

I read Isaac's book at night with a flashlight because Mom and Dad probably wouldn't approve of me reading it. There are drug dealers and pool sharks in it and other sketchy characters. The book isn't bad, except that every few chapters the lawyer lady hero gives a speech, either about civil rights, or men needing to treat women better, or jazz being better than disco. The book ends with the promise of more Billie Ruth books.

"Have you ever heard of Margaret Ruth Biddle?" I ask Mom and Dad on the way home. "That's Isaac's mother." The book is dedicated to her and that reminded me of Yolanda talking about her like I should know who she is.

"There's a school named for her," Mom says.

"Oh yeah." That's why the name rings a bell!

When we get into cell phone range I ask Google to tell me more about her. It brings up a Wikipedia page! I've never known someone with their own Wikipedia page, unless you count Cyrus Popp. I scan it and read the highlights to Mom and Dad.

"It says Margaret Ruth Biddle was born in Chicago in 1919.

Not much is known about her early life, but she ended up in Minneapolis as a single mother in 1936. She worked as a hotel maid and took night classes at the Girls Vocational College."

"*Girls* Vocational College," my mother echoes in horror. "*College* is for adults! *Vocations* are for adults!"

"It was the 1930s," Dad says with a shrug. "They used to...."

"I know they used to." Mom gives him a look and Dad stops mid-sentence. I plunge back in.

"It says she worked as a legal secretary until her child was grown. That means she worked for a law firm, not that there are also *illegal* secretaries."

"We know, Lucas," Mom says with a laugh.

"Some people don't," I tell her. "Anyway, it says in the 1950s she started taking classes at the William Mitchell School of Law and became one of the first black female attorneys in Minnesota. And then she became the first black woman in the state to be a full partner at a law firm. She specialized in defending minority clients who were being treated unfairly by the legal system, but she later quit being a defense lawyer to fight for equality in housing and employment. And then there's a bunch of stuff about that. She got something called a J.D. and lectured at William Mitchell after she retired."

"A juris doctorate *and* an activist? Wow, Isaac's mom sounds like a hero," Dad says.

"No wonder they named a school after her," Mom says. "Isaac must be so proud."

"Yeah," I agree. I realize that Billie Ruth is obviously based on his mother. I start to tell Mom and Dad about the book but stop. They might want to read it, and then they might get mad that I read a book with drug dealers and pool sharks.

"He must have a lot of stories," Dad says.

"I'm sure he does," Mom says. "Hmm, I wonder how he's doing?"

"Me too," I tell her. I think about calling the hospital but decide to wait until we get home.

• • •

There are two pieces of good news on voice mail. One is that Dad has a second job interview. The other is that Isaac is home!

"He's still recovering, and he'll need therapy for many weeks," Yolanda's message says. "I'll be staying with him, but can you come by once a day and relieve me?"

It's already late in the day when we get the message, but I make a note to go over tomorrow.

Meanwhile, the *Smashtown Frenzy* tour has moved on to Dallas and Houston, but people are still complaining about the Minneapolis tournament.

What's the point? one comment says on Cyrus's recap of the final round in Dallas. *Everybody knows it's fixed. The kids in Minny are scripted to win. Why else would Cyrus feature them before they even played?*

The other team just SAT THERE AND WAITED TO LOSE, another commenter says. *WHY WOULD THEY DO THAT UNLESS THEY WERE THROWING THE MATCH.* Followed by a row of white flag emojis to drive home the point.

There are more comments like that, a lot of them in all-caps, a lot of them with strings of emojis. I scroll down and that's all I see. I'm sure there are a few that say otherwise, but if so, they are lost in the flood of skepticism and conspiracy theories.

My phone buzzes. It's Max. Actually calling, not texting.

"Hey," I answer.

"Have you seen all the stuff?" he asks. I know right away what he means by "stuff."

"Yep."

"Some people want drama," he says. "That's what Tori says."

"Yeah." So the teammate who ditched us a week before the tournament thinks *other* people want drama?

"She says not to take it personally."

"I know, I know." I don't take it personally, but I *am* worried about walking into Chicago with everyone hating on us. I can handle losing. Losing is part of the game. But all the booing and name-calling is hard to stomach. I remember the vibe on the first day of the tournament, like everybody was united by our love for *Smashtown* games. It was a warm, wonderful feeling. How could *winning* have ruined that?

"Do you want to play now?" I ask him. "Not official team practice. Just to play?"

"Heck, yeah. Tori can play too."

"I'll text Noah."

We form a new squad with the classic lineup, call ourselves the Hotdogs, and smash some noobs. It feels so good to be

Trunky again, stomping my way through the streets I know so well. It even feels good to have Tori back on the team and calling the shots, even though she bailed on us. Her team losing the tourney while we move on feels like enough payback for that. It feels even better to play without performing, with no audience and no pressure.

"Guess we'll play tomorrow," I say over the game channel before we quit for the night. "We should practice."

"'Cept for me," Tori reminds me.

"Right. Sorry."

"Let's start early," Max says. "Like nine?"

"Nope, I can't." I have to see Isaac. I've never told the other 4LMNTs about Senior Sitters. It felt like a lot to explain and we were always focused on the tournament. "Noon?"

"Fine," Max says, but he doesn't sound like it's fine at all.

• • •

The next morning there's a thunderstorm, the kind that turns the streets into rivers. I'd wanted to cycle over to Isaac's, but there's no way I can ride through the driving rain. Dad can't take me because he's about to leave for his job interview.

"Hope it lets up soon," he says, watching the raindrops bouncing off the sidewalk. "I don't want to show up soaked." Our garage isn't attached to the house, and the wind is the kind that turns umbrellas inside out.

"They'll be wet too," I point out.

"Good point," he says with a smile, but he sounds nervous.

He pulls on a clear plastic poncho over his suit jacket and tie and walks out the back, taking careful steps down the flooded path so he won't splash his pants cuffs. A moment later the car backs out of the driveway and rolls through the small lake at the end of the street, the tires sending up little tidal waves.

• • •

Max isn't online, so I go to Streamcast, forgetting for a few seconds that it's turned into a hate-fest for my team. Cyrus has posted a short video entitled "Cyrus Responds to the Skeptics." The video looks like it was made in a hotel room using his phone.

"Look everyone," he says, forgetting the usual Cyborg greeting. His tone is tired and serious. "I've been reading your comments about the *Smashtown Frenzy* tournament in Minneapolis." He shakes his head in disbelief. "First of all, this competition is totally, one hundred percent, legit. Second, I've replayed the matches from Minneapolis and so should you. You will see that the kids who won are smart, skilled players. They harassed the other team, got under their skin, and forced them into some bad decisions. That is *not* dumb luck. I was mistaken. Finally, and most importantly, I don't care if people talk trash to me, but don't talk trash to these young players. Come on, Cyborgs. Last year these kids were playing *Paw Patrol: On a Roll!*" He shakes his head again, mutters goodbye, and signs off.

So *he's* on our side, sort of. The *Paw Patrol* crack stings a little.

• • •

Not sure I can make it but I can play from here, I text Max.

Bummer. Wait. A moment later he follows up. *Tori's boyfriend's mom can drive you.*

Tori has a BOYFRIEND?

Well, she's been hanging out with a guy she met when we were at the cabin. He'll be in 10th grade. He is coming and sez he can give u a ride. His name is Jacob. You know him.

I do?

You'll see. Gave him your addy. He'll pick you up at noon.

I haven't had lunch. I dig through the fridge in search of olives and find none, but we do have cream cheese and pickles. I make a sandwich on whole grain bread and eat it in a hurry. I pack up my laptop and pull a plastic bag over it to make it more waterproof before I shove it into my backpack. I watch through the front windows until I see a sporty SUV come slowly up the street, wending around the bigger puddles. I go outside and wave. The car stops. I lock the door behind me and run out into the rain. It hasn't let up a bit. There's a stressed-out looking woman in the driver's seat and a high-school kid in the passenger seat. He waves at me, so I climb into the back.

"Thanks for picking me up!" I figure the woman is stressed from driving in the rain.

"Hey, Lucas," the kid says. "We met at the tournament? I'm Jacob."

"Oh right." I probably look like a cartoon character whose eyes turn as wide as plates and pop out of their sockets. Tori's new pal is the well-dressed, curly haired kid from SLP. The leader of the team we beat in the final.

• • •

"So the Nelsons have a cabin near ours on Leech Lake," Max explains as we set up to play. Tori and Jacob are in the living room and we're in the dining room. "And Jacob is friends with one of their kids, so he was there, and Tori recognized him from the tournament and she went over to talk to him."

"But you didn't recognize him?" I ask.

"Not at first. I mostly know him as a snake. I don't mean that's *he's* a snake, but you know. Anyway, they're into the same stuff besides *Smashtown*. Like Neil Gaiman and Imagine Dragons. He's all right when you get to know him."

"And now they're *dating?*"

"Not really. Mom wouldn't allow it anyway. But it's weird for me that suddenly Tori is hanging out with high school guys."

"She's in high school herself," I remind him.

"Not yet," he says. "Not until September."

Max and Tori get along better than most siblings I know. They're actual pals. I think he's a little sad she's leaving Fremont and hanging out with new friends. On the other hand, she's hanging out with kids her own age instead of us. She didn't have a lot of friends until recently. She was too geeky for other girls at Fremont, into all the wrong things. Even though she bailed on our team, I guess I kind of get why she did it.

"You know, about Tori—" Max starts to say, but then Zach comes in, dripping from the rain. He sets his bag down to take off his raincoat, scattering droplets everywhere.

"Sheesh, be careful," Max says.

"Sorry." He looks around for a place to put the wet coat and hangs the hood from a knob on the back of a chair. "Did you know the enemy has infiltrated your home?" he asks, pointing toward the living room dramatically.

"Jacob is an *opponent*, not an enemy," Max says. "And he hasn't *infiltrated* anything, Tori invited him."

"I think the enemy has gotten to him," Zach stage whispers to me. Max rolls his eyes.

Noah comes in a moment later, *not* dripping water or carrying his raincoat. He left it on the porch like a civilized person.

"Hey, guys. Ready to smash noobs?"

"That's why we're here," Max says.

"Hey, before I forget, I need a ride to Chicago," Noah says to Max. "Can I go with you guys?"

"I'll ask my parents. We can get five into my dad's CRV. You might even be able stay at my grandma's house in Naperville."

"That would be awesome."

We hear Tori guffawing from the living room. I've never heard her laugh like that. Either Jacob is hilarious, or she's faking it because she likes him. Maybe a bit of both.

"Infiltrated," Zach says under his breath.

• • •

We spend the next hour or two smashing noobs. It's fun but it's too easy. The tournament has gotten even more kids excited about the game, so there are a lot more new players, and most haven't figured out basic strategy. In some cases they don't even know how to use the controls. We win matches where the other team is literally running into walls and one another.

"None of these teams are as good as the ones we'll see in Chicago," Noah says.

"So, we need to play a good team," I tell him.

"We could play Tori's team," Max says. "MadMachine actually *beat* us. Nobody else did."

"Ugh, don't remind me," Zach says.

"But you can only invite teams to play you if you're both on the leaderboard," I remind them. "And we can't seem to get back on the leaderboard." I leave off the next thought, which is that it's because of Zach. Our team XP is way down because his XP is a lot lower than ours.

"The leaderboard is a joke," Noah says. We all saucer-eye at him. The leaderboard? Before the tournament, it was the only goal any of us had. "Well, it is!" he says. "It's more about quantity play than quality play."

I know what he means. It's cumulative. The more matches you win, the more points your team has. But it can be a whole lot of matches against guys who run into walls. I guess the main reason we can't get back on the leaderboard is, is because of all the kids out there with parents who let them play twenty-four seven to rack up points.

"Exactly," says Max, "But we can play on a dedicated server."

"What?" Zach squints at him.

"You can access a dedicated server, like in *Minecraft* or *Fortnite*." Max logs out and then angles the screen so we can see it. "Did you never notice this?"

There are the username and password boxes to log in, the

small button to create a new account, and, on the lower right, a little icon in the shape of a key. Max clicks it. A pop-up asks us for a code.

"Oh, I've clicked that," I tell them. "But I didn't know what it meant or how it works."

"Neither do I," Max says. "But I know someone who probably does."

"Tori," Noah and I guess at the same time. She's the techie among us.

"Jinx, buy me a Coke!" Zach throws in a split-second later.

"Dude, you didn't say the thing at the same time we did," Noah tells him.

"You still owe me a Coke because I said *jinx* first," Zach insists.

"That's not how it works!" I say.

"There's soda in the fridge," Max says as he stands up. "Let's talk to Tori."

• • •

"You can't just hack into a dedicated server," she tells us. "You need an access code."

"And where do you get the code?" Noah asks. Tori shrugs and looks at Jacob.

"Oh, I know people," Jacob says coolly.

"Streamcast stars?" I ask.

"Sure. And game reviewers."

"And his dad," Tori says.

"And my dad," Jacob admits.

"No kidding? Why does he have access?"

"His company manages the commerce integration for Kogeki in North America. Sometimes they beta test new skins and stuff. Anything you buy, my dad made it happen."

"Wow!" Max says. "That is so awesome."

It is. Jacob is now officially the coolest person I know. Besides Cyrus Popp, of course. I mean, actually developing the game would be a million times cooler than *commerce integration*, but I bet his dad actually hangs with the developers.

"Do *you* have the code?" Max asks.

"I could probably get it," he says.

"Would we get in big trouble for using it?" Noah asks. "I mean, like, banned from the game?"

"Nah," Jacob says. "It's not that big a deal. You're playing the same game, you just get to pick your opponents. And sometimes see stuff in beta."

"So we can have a rematch anytime?" I suggest.

"I guess so, but I think that should wait until August." He gives me a sideways look. "Why would you want a rematch anyway? You won."

"Because we need to practice," I tell him. "I read that Minneapolis was the smallest competition in the tournament. Which also makes it the easiest. Which means we'll face better teams in Chicago than we did here."

"It's simple statistics," Noah agrees.

Jacob sits up straight, suddenly alert.

"Really? You think so?"

"Really," I tell him.

"Ah, I'm not worried."

"Dude, you lost to *us*," I tell him.

"I kind of let you win," he says. Which is sort of true and sort of not true. Jacob lets out a long breath. "Maybe we *could* set up a few practice sessions. But we can't keep playing each other. That might be worse than not practicing at all."

"MadMachine can play you guys," Tori offers. "We beat the guys who beat you." She grins at Jacob, but he doesn't take the bait.

"I know the Sigh Borgs," he says. "They're as good as any of us." He looks thoughtful for a moment. "Let's do this."

CHAPTER 8

I bike over to Isaac's the next morning, rolling through puddles that slosh up on my legs. As I knock, I feel even more nervous than I did the first time I came alone. I don't know what kind of shape Isaac will be in. Yolanda answers the door.

"It's your friend Lucas," she announces. "He's the one who—"

"I know who Lucas is," Isaac says crossly.

I see Isaac in his favorite chair. He looks like he always does. Maybe a bit tired, but not as bad as I feared.

"I wanted to come yesterday, but there was the storm and my dad couldn't take me," I explain. He glances up at me but seems to have trouble focusing.

"Do you want to listen to one of those Ross Cooper books?" I ask.

"Sure," he says with a nod.

"I'll do the cat boxes first." I set my backpack by the chair I usually use and head for the basement. Yolanda stops me in the kitchen. She puts a hand on my shoulder, cranes her neck to peer into the living room, then whispers.

"You need to know a few things."

"Yeah?"

"He has short-term memory loss. He knows who he is and what happened. But he might forget what you told him a few minutes ago. And he's short-tempered. It's like the filter is gone. That's all normal for someone who's been through what he has. But you should know he might behave differently than you're used to."

"OK. Thanks for the warning."

"I need to get groceries and a prescription for him," she says. "Can you stay with him until I get back? It won't be more than an hour."

"Sure. No problem."

"Thank you. Thank you." She heads out after telling Isaac she'll be back soon. I go downstairs.

The smell in the basement nearly knocks me over. It's been a week since the boxes have been scooped, and the midsummer humidity has made the sand gray and clumpy. On top of that, the cats have been busy. I change the boxes completely and haul the bags of used litter out back.

When I return to the living room, Isaac looks at me with wide, confused eyes.

"Lucas," I remind him. "I'm from Senior Sitters."

"I know that!" he snaps. Sam the cat has been curled peacefully in his lap, but Isaac's sudden outburst makes him scamper down and across the room.

"I didn't know you were still here," he then says in a normal voice. Sam climbs up into another chair and looks at him with what I think is concern.

"Sorry to freak you out. I was downstairs a long time."

I want to change the mood, and I remember something. "Hey! I read one of your books." I zip open my backpack and take out *She's on the Case.* "It's really good! I want to read the rest of the books about Billie Ruth."

He takes a long time to say anything.

"Where'd you get that?"

"Uh . . ." I set the book on the coffee table and hope that speaks for itself. I don't want him to be mad at me for borrowing it.

"Did I lend you that?"

"Not exactly," I admit. "I saw your name on it and wanted to read it."

"I thought I burned every last copy," he says and shakes his head sadly.

"It says there would be more books about Billie Ruth," I say finally. "Are there? I would *read* more."

"Nope, that's the only one," he says. "The publisher didn't want more because nobody bought that one." He nods grimly at the book. "You might as well keep it."

"Thanks." I take the book back off the table. I want to say something positive. "It led me to reading about your mom," I tell him. "She was really amazing."

"Yes she was," he says without much enthusiasm.

"She must have been really proud of you. For writing

this book." I hold it up for emphasis.

"She hated it," he says sadly.

"Gosh. I'm sorry." I try to imagine a world where I publish a book and my parents aren't proud of me, even if it was *A Gamer's Guide to Smashing Noobs*. I can't.

I've got nothing else to say, and neither does he. We forget all about the audiobook. I want to leave, but I promised Yolanda I'd wait for her to get back. So we sit in the gloomy house, barely looking at each other and not talking, until she bangs back through the front door, arms full of groceries. I escape as soon as I can.

• • •

Dad drives the four of us to Jacob's house for gaming practice; I ride shotgun while Max, Noah, and Zach cram into the back. The house is down a winding road near Lake Minnetonka.

"Nice digs," Dad says when he sees the white stone house and massive lawn, cradled by a copse of trees.

"You're not a *KidfromSLP*," I chide as Jacob leads us down into the finished basement. We're in Minnetonka. Technically, he lives just a couple miles from St. Louis Park, but it feels like we're in another world.

"Our school's in SLP," he explains.

"Holy cow!" Zach stares in wonder at Jacob's basement. He stops to ogle a huge aquarium with a variety of fish. "Do your fish have names?"

"Yeah, but they never come when you call them," Jacob says dryly.

"And you have a foosball table!" Zach drops a ball and gives one row of players a twirl to kick it but moves on before he sees what happens. "You have a refrigerator downstairs?" He opens it and gapes at the sodas.

"Help yourself," Jacob says. Zach grabs a Mountain Dew and splonks it open.

"Sorry," Noah whispers to Jacob. "I don't think he gets out much."

More high school kids come tramping down the steps: the rest of Jacob's team, followed by the girl twins from the Sigh Borgs. All of them are toting laptops. I learn that the girl twins are Lia and Mia. I note that Lia has studs in her ears and Mia wears dangling hoops. That's how I'll tell them apart. The rest of Jacob's team are Emily, Chloe, and Nash. Even though they are mix of girls and boys and Nash is black, they blur as much as the twins. They're all so preppy, with tidy hair and dressy-casual clothes.

"Where's everyone going to sit?" Mia asks.

"I could dig out the tables and chairs we use on holidays," Jacob says. "Champs, help me out here?" I realize he means the 4LMNTs. We follow him into a side room and carry out card tables and folding chairs. Meanwhile, the other Sigh Borgs and MadMachine arrive. I still don't know everyone's name on Tori's team.

Soon we're all set up: MadMachine on the couch and chairs, the Sigh Borgs sitting on pillows around the coffee table, and the two other teams at card tables. Jacob hands out power strips and long orange extension cords, one per team.

"I made the Wi-Fi public so you should get online, no problem. Last but not least, the access code. When you go to log in, click the key icon and type this in." He gives a card to Tori. She taps on her keyboard and passes the card along to Madison. It takes a while to get to us, and when I finally get the card it's like being handed a golden ticket to a magical chocolate factory. It has a string of twenty letters and numbers neatly printed in ink. I click the key on the login page and tap it in. I see a list of active servers, strings of letters, numbers, and periods.

"What now?"

"Click the first one and wait until everyone's in," Jacob says.

As soon as everyone's done, Jacob whisks the card away. "All right," he says. "Time to battle."

"Let's smash some noobs!" Zach says, but none of our opponents are noobs, and we're the ones who get smashed. In the first match, we play the Sigh Borgs, who have changed their lineup. They kept one Leothrawl and one Kwill, but they've added a tank—Trunkzilla, how I've missed him!—and Raptora, an eagle with a mighty wind flap that sends opponents reeling. They win easily. After that we face MadMachine, playing with Zigzap, Pugiless the boxing kangaroo, Bizzard, and a bison tank named Buffle. It's a complete change from the first match; the first was long and hard, but this one is over before we can figure out a strategy. After a few more losses I sense that the older kids are looking at us sideways, wondering how they lost to us in the tournament.

We take a break. Jacob pours a bag of popcorn into a bowl, opens a box of cookies, and tells everyone to help themselves to drinks. It's really grown up, the way he hosts a gaming session. Zach is the first to the fridge to grab another Dew. Max and Noah head to the foosball table. The KidsfromSLP talk about the matches and how they might have played them better. So far, they're undefeated. MadMachine talks in low voices with Lia and Mia from the Sigh Borgs, either about the matches or high school girl stuff. The other half of the Sigh Borgs, Owen and Oliver, look at their phones. Neither of them is a big talker.

Zach finds the remote to the TV and turns it on.

"Cool, you can watch Streamcast on your TV! My mom refuses to buy a smart TV." He taps a button and Jacob's homepage comes up, a feed full of gaming channels I don't watch because they're about games I don't play. Zach taps the microphone button on the remote and says "Cyrus Popp," His channel comes up. A new video is posted called "Big News Before ABQ."

"Oh great," says Mia dryly. "Cyrus *Plllopp*." She drags out the L sound.

"I hope his big news is that he's retiring from making videos forever," says Lia.

I know a lot of kids dump on Cyrus, maybe because he's so popular.

"What's wrong with Cyrus? He's awesome." Zach looks to me for support, knowing I'm a fan. But I want the girls to think I'm cool, so I shrug.

"He's all right," I say mildly. The girls trade a glance.

Zach hits play on the video. It's another from a hotel room, but this one's framed better and has better lighting.

"Greetings, Cyborgs!" Cyrus says. "Albuquerque promises to be as hot as Phoenix, gamewise *and* temperature wise. But I've got big news that is not about the tournament. I have the exclusive world premiere trailer of a new *Smashtown* game from Kogeki Games. That's right, Cyborgs. The makers of *Smashtown Frontiers* and *Smashtown Frenzy* have a new game, and you're going to see a sneak preview right here, right now!"

The screen cuts to *Smashtown*. I can tell it's *Smashtown* by the style, but it's an area I've never seen before. The camera zeros in on a silver box perched on top of a ruined water tower, then pans to the ground. A saber-toothed tiger and boar are stalking through a wasteland. The tiger points to the top of the tower and the boar nods. Both are new characters. The camera scales back and you see a dozen other characters also preparing to scale the tower. Some new characters, some old characters. There's not even enough time to take it all in. The screen turns black, and three-dimensional words slide *Star Wars* style across the screen.

NEW MISSIONS.

NEW TERRITORY.

NEW CHARACTERS.

NEW BATTLES.

And then a second-long video of the tiger lady and her piggy pal jumping into the fray before the screen goes black again.

SMASHTOWN FURY.

AUGUST 28.

"Whoooooa!" Zach says in awe.

"Ah, they finally dropped that ad," Jacob says knowingly.

Cyrus is back on the screen.

"Believe your eyes, Cyborgs! Some brand-new Smashtown content is coming in a few weeks, and of course you'll see *live* game play the moment it's released, right here on this channel. I'm so excited I'm stroking out!" He does his trademark bit. I hadn't thought about it since Isaac had his stroke, and suddenly it feels really . . . wrong.

"Me too!" Zach says and plays along. I glance around and see Noah and Max doing it. Nash is doing it too. Even Tori and Madison are doing it. It's like every other person in the room is stroking out.

I think of Isaac stumbling around his house with his sagging face and weak arms. It looked completely different from what Cyrus is doing. I mean, I knew strokes probably didn't really look like that, but it didn't seem to matter before. Now it hits me like a stealth attack.

I back up and find an edge of the couch between Lia and Mia.

"Hey!" Lia says. Then, realizing something is wrong, she asks "Are you all right?"

"I think *he's* stroking out," jokes Owen.

The moment passes. "No, no. I'm fine," I tell them. "It's

just . . . that stroke thing he does is really not funny." I take a deep breath. "Someone I know had a stroke. It's really serious."

"It is," Lia says. I glance at her and see sympathy in her eyes. She's wearing a summery blue blouse with a white print. It's something a rich woman would wear to the country club. Suddenly I'm hyper-aware that my shorts and legs are muddy from this morning's bike ride, and that I haven't clipped my fingernails since before our vacation.

"Ah, come on. Grow a sense of humor," Nash says.

"Yeah, lighten up," says Owen.

"You did the stroke bit yourself," Max reminds me. "In that video with Cy."

"It's true. You did." Noah nods at me.

"I know," I admit in a low voice, feeling kind of sick. *But that was before.*

"I can bring it up right now!" says Zach, grabbing the remote.

"It's fine. You don't have to. I know it happened." But Zach has already tapped the microphone button.

"Cyrus Popp, *Smashtown* Tournament, Minneapolis," he says carefully, so the speech recognition can pick up the words. A moment later the screen shows the four of us at the hot-dog truck. Zach zips to the end of the video and freezes the frame with our faces mid-boil.

"See?"

"Lovely," Lia says, glancing at me with disappointment.

"Big deal," says Nash. "Everybody thinks they have to be offended by everything these days. It's ridiculous."

"I'm not offended," I say weakly. "But that's not what strokes look like and it's not funny."

"The shtick *is* played out," Jacob says agreeably. "Come on, let's game."

• • •

"They offered me the job!" Dad announces at dinner. "I start on Monday. I'm going in tomorrow to do HR paperwork and get my access card. It's moving fast."

"I knew you would get it!" Mom says.

"That's awesome, Dad!"

We're having chicken tacos. The shell is cracked on mine, and the juice is sluicing down my arm. I grab at a napkin and try to dab it off.

"It's a step up," Dad continues. "More than I got paid before, and better benefits. It's pretty corporate for me, but the people seem nice. It's a big relief to have found something. But, uh." He looks at me. "I'm not eligible for vacation time for three months, and there's a big project that has to be done by the end of August." I'm still trying to salvage my leaky taco, and I'm not connecting the dots with what Dad's saying. "So . . . I'm afraid I can't take you to Chicago," he finishes gravely.

"What?" I drop the balled-up napkin on the table.

"Sorry, buddy. It took me months to find a job, and I want to start out on the right foot."

I look at Mom in desperation.

"You know I can't take that week off," she says. "That's the end of our fiscal year. I have massive budget work to do. That's why I wasn't going with you two in the first place."

"But how am I supposed to get to the tournament?" My voice is an octave higher than usual.

"Maybe you can go with one of your friends?" Mom suggests.

"Maybe." But Max's folks are already giving a ride to Noah, I remember. Which means their car is full. Maybe I can ride with Zach's family?

"Sorry, kiddo," Dad says. "It's not ideal, but we have to prioritize."

Everything is going wrong. Everybody in Chicago will be rooting against us from the second we enter the building. The 4LMNTs are in a slump; we got trounced all afternoon. Now I might not even be able to *go* to the tournament. Isaac is hurting and I don't know how to help him. On top of all that, my taco is broken. The unfairness of it all is too much to take. I push the plate away and stomp upstairs to my room, using a few of the worst words I know. I slam the door and lock it for good measure.

I expect Mom or Dad to come after me to ask if everything is all right (it isn't) or tell me I'm too old to act like this (I am). But neither does either. I'm all alone to stew in my misfortune, but self-pity is boring. I flip on my laptop and check my feed. Every single post is about the new *Smashtown* game. At least nobody's talking about us anymore.

I follow a few links but nobody knows anything more than what was in the trailer.

I replay the Cyrus Popp announcement so I can see the

trailer again, scanning for details I overlooked the first time. I see a giant worm character I'd missed before. And an elaborate compound surrounded by barbed wire fences, protected by big dogs. The new stuff looks darker than the usual *Smashtown* missions.

I feel that impatient thrill I always do when I see a new game but can't play it yet.

But I cringe when Cyrus does his stroke bit at the end of the trailer. I can't do anything about Dad's new job or us getting trounced in the tournament, but maybe I can do something about this.

I used to leave comments on Cyrus's videos, but they always got lost in the flood so I stopped. I start to type one now.

Cyrus, I'm a big fan and I'm excited for the new Smashtown game. Thanks for showing the trailer! But I wonder if you can stop it with the stroke joke. I remember Jacob's words and write, *That shtick is played out.* That sounds cool and laid back, but it misses the point. I delete it and try again. *If you saw somebody have a stroke, you'd know it's not like that and it's not funny.* Now it's to the point, but I know people will mock me. Streamcast is brutal.

There's a knock on my door.

"Kiddo?" It's Dad. "Do you want to come eat your dinner before I scrape the plate into the compost bin?"

"I don't know," I tell him, which is true. I am hungry, but I can't eat.

"Ah," Dad says. "Look, I'm really sorry about your tournament. Your mother and I know how important it is to you. I wish there was a way to make it work with my new job."

"I know," I tell him. "Sorry I stomped up the stairs and everything."

"I get it. It was hard news. But we don't talk to *you* like that, so please don't make a habit of it."

"I won't."

"We'll give you fifteen minutes, then the tacos get dumped. They don't keep well or I'd put them in the fridge." I hear his footsteps treading away.

I delete my comment on Cyrus Popp's video, and struggle to find the right words. Probably Cyrus won't see it anyway, I think. I notice the option to post a video reply. Nobody posts video replies except for Streamcast noobs and streamers trying to drive traffic to their own gaming channels. I decide to give it a try. I hit the reply-by-video button, angle the camera at myself, adjust the desk light, and click the red circle to begin.

"Hi, Cy, this is Lucas of the 4LMNTs, the team that won the Minneapolis tournament?" I remember that Cyrus likes us and that makes me less nervous. "Hey, thanks for sticking up for us the other day. But I actually want to tell you what happened *after* the tournament." I tell him about dropping in on Isaac, realizing that something was wrong, and calling 911. I tell him what the lady at 911 told me about strokes. I talk about Isaac, how he now looks crumpled and can't remember stuff that happened five minutes ago. How he might never be the same again.

"So strokes are serious," I tell the camera. "I used to think that stroke bit was funny, but now that I've seen what they really are, I've changed my mind. Probably lots of your fans have friends and family who've had strokes, and it makes them feel bad to see you making fun of it." I hit stop. I feel like I did well. I should probably watch the video before I submit, but it's been almost fifteen minutes so I hit send and run downstairs to save my tacos.

CHAPTER 9

I take a long shower the next morning, clip my nails, and carefully pick my clothes to exude a Jacob-style preppy confidence: dark green golf shorts (I've never golfed) and a cream-colored polo shirt (I've never played polo either). I put on sandals, then swap them out for ankle socks and sneaks, then try the sandals again, then try the shoes again with different socks. I wish I had the kind of low-cut deck shoes Jacob wears. I end up with the sandals. My sneaks are too beaten up.

"Why are you all gussied up?" Dad asks. Dad is old even for a dad, like twelve years older than my mom, and says stuff like "gussied up." He is dressed up too, since he's going to his new job.

"I'm not that gussied," I protest. "I dress like this all the time."

"Sure you do," he says. "So, uh, are there any girls at these gaming practices?"

"A few." I will my face to stay the same color.

"Are you going to see Isaac this morning?" he asks.

"Oh yeah." I haven't forgotten about Isaac, but I hadn't thought about the bike ride. The ride in the humid air would make me grubby and ruin the whole effect, and I wouldn't have time to shower and change before practice. "I'll see if I can go after practice," I tell Dad.

"Hope whoever it is appreciates you going the extra mile." He gives me a wink and heads out.

I send a text to Yolanda asking if it's OK to come later in the day because of the heat.

Sure, she messages back. *We have an appt at 2, back around 4. Stay cool!*

I eat breakfast and turn on my computer. I have time to kill, since we're not meeting until after lunch, and since I'm not going to Isaac's.

My feed is full of notifications:

Bubblesnot replied to your comment.

Goober78 replied to your comment.

DredFossil replied to your comment.

It takes me a moment to realize what they're talking about. The video reply I left for Cyrus. I gulp and click the button to bring up the replies.

Most of the comments are the "u r dum" variety. Some of the haters have even clicked through to my channel and left snarky comments and down votes on my old videos (more down voters than people who watched the videos, I can tell from the stats). That's Streamcast. Somebody could post a video of Abraham Lincoln reciting the Gettysburg Address and half the comments would say "u r dum." I don't let it get to me. OK, it gets to me a *little*. But only a little.

• • •

"You trying out for Jacob's new BFF?" Max asks me when he sees my golf shorts and polo shirt. We're meeting at his house to get a ride to Jacob's for practice.

"Nah, he's auditioning to be a mannequin at L.L. Bean," Noah says.

"No, no," Zach jumps in. "Uh, he wants . . ." His eyes roll to the ceiling as he tries to think of something witty. "He's got a new job as our school principal!"

"Then he needs a tie with Minions on it," Max says with a laugh. The principal wears a lot of goofy ties, like he wants the parents to know he's serious enough to wear a tie but also wants the kids to think he's cool.

"Stop making fun of me or you all have detention!" I order. I'm glad none of them suggest my clothes have anything to do with Lia, which I would deny anyway.

• • •

"Lookin' spiffy, Lukezilla," Jacob says when we get to his house.

"You know my Streamcast name?"

"Yes, I saw your comment on the *Fury* trailer," he says as we head downstairs. I wait for further feedback, which he doesn't give.

"What did it say?" Lia glances my way. I no longer need the earrings to tell her apart from her sister. Today she's wearing a shimmery blue-green skirt and a matching top. Still very much in the grown-up/country-club style. Mia is wearing a retro *Space Invaders* T-shirt and jean shorts. They really don't look *that* much alike, I realize.

"He said strokes aren't funny," Jacob says evenly.

"Hmm," says Lia. "Well, they aren't."

"Anything can be funny," Nash argues.

"But *Cyrus* isn't funny," says Mia.

"I like Cyrus Popp," I admit. "I just don't like *that* bit. *Anymore*," I add, since everybody saw me do it.

"Well," Jacob rubs his hands. "This is a fascinating topic, but we should start practicing."

We 4LMNTs do better today, taking three of the first five matches. The losses are close, and one of our wins is a landslide. I hear either Oliver or Owen wail, "Noooooo!" as their wall comes tumbling down.

During the first break, Lia sees me by the fridge. She talks in a low voice as she twists the top off her fizzy water.

"I just watched your video on my phone. Our uncle had a heart attack last Christmas. I know it's not the same thing as a stroke, but I get where you're coming from."

"Thanks," I manage to say without stammering.

"What you did . . . ," she says. "It was necessary. And brave." She lays a cool hand on my arm, which I feel for the rest of the afternoon.

Brave? That's the word I wonder about. Why was it brave

unless there were risks involved? Why was it brave unless making that video was a lot stupider than I imagined?

· · ·

"I need a ride to Chicago," I mention on the ride back to Minneapolis, since Max's mom is driving.

"We already agreed to take Noah," she says. "We can only fit five safely." She doesn't officially say no but lets me draw the necessary conclusion. There's no room for me.

Max nudges me.

"Dude, how can you still be working out a ride?" he whispers.

"My dad got a new job," I explain. I look at Zach, who doesn't look back. He is my last-ditch hope. He's watching the blur of orange pylons and piles of dirt on the side of the road—a work crew is there—and pretending he doesn't hear us. He's going to force me to ask.

"Zach, how are you getting to Chicago?"

Max elbows me. I look at him and he mouths something I don't pick up. It looks like "Don't," but don't what? I need a ride and his mother just said it couldn't be with them.

"Zach?"

"Huh?" He finally turns back to face us. "What?"

"How are you getting to Chicago? For the tournament finals?" I ask him.

"Oh yeah. That."

"Do you have a ride to Chicago?"

"So, the thing is, my mom . . ." His voice rings on, but to

me he sounds like a cartoon dog in this viral video. *Ba ba ba ba. Ba ba ba, ba ba ba.*

The gist of it is, he does not have a ride. He never did have a ride and has not been figuring out a ride. Which means half our team doesn't have a ride. Which means we might be out of the tournament before it begins.

• • •

"Don't you look smart," Yolanda says when I get to Isaac's house late that afternoon.

"Thanks." I peer past her into the darkness. "How's he doing?"

"Therapy is hard," she whispers. "He's napping now. I should go home for a while, but I'll be back to bring him dinner. I'm glad you're here to keep him company."

"Is he still mad at me?" I whisper back.

"Why would he be mad at you?" She tilts her head and squints at me.

"I read his book. The one he wrote."

"I didn't know *that* was the book you were borrowing." She shakes her head.

"Is he upset that the book didn't sell well or something?"

"There's more to it than that," she says. "It got bad reviews, and he felt rejected. But the worst part was that his mother *hated* it. She saw it. . . . Well, she thought he was mocking her. It was the end of their relationship. Mind you, it wasn't that great a relationship anyway." She's talked herself short of breath and stops to catch it. "Well, you know I love and admire Maggie Ruth more than any person I've known, but she was always hard on Isaac. And I wasn't able to talk her into forgiving him for that book."

"But he doesn't need to be forgiven. He didn't do anything wrong," I protest.

"She doesn't see it that way," Yolanda says. "I mean, I agree, but nobody can convince Maggie Ruth of anything when she's made up her mind."

Margaret Ruth Biddle was amazing, but she apparently had a dark side.

"Isaac wants to see her," Yolanda says. "He says he better visit her before he dies. I tell him he's not dying any time soon, but he's right. We should visit."

"Where is she buried?" I ask. "Can I go with you two?"

Yolanda tilts her head at me. "She's not *buried* anywhere, Lucas! She's as alive as you and me."

"What?! His mother is still alive? She must be like a hundred years old!"

"Ninety-eight," Yolanda says. "Ninety-nine in January."

"Holy cow. Where does she live?"

"Chicago," Yolanda says. "She went home in 2000 to help take care of her sister when she was dying. She never moved back. We talk on the phone sometimes, but I haven't seen her in almost twenty years and neither has Isaac. I think it's time we fixed that. She lives in a senior center there. It'll be a tough time for Isaac to take a trip, but . . . Well, we can't wait any longer."

"I want to go!" I tell her. I'm not even thinking about

the tournament. I want to meet the legendary Margaret Ruth Biddle. But I think of the tournament a split second later. "I mean, can I please go too?" I ask more nicely. "And can I bring a friend?"

PART 2
CHICAGO

CHAPTER 10

There are entire Streamcast channels where musicians imitate popular songs with new lyrics about video games. Zach spends the entire drive to Chicago finding and playing these songs on his phone. He's wearing headphones, but I can hear the tinny rhythms while Zach bops and gestures in his seat. He adds to the percussion by either chomping on hot Cheetos or smacking watermelon-flavored gum, which mixes in a way that would give Squunk a run for his stinky money. Unfortunately, Yolanda has a car with a USB charging port in the back, so there's no hope Zach's phone battery will drain. Also, unfortunately, Zach looks well stocked on gum and Cheetos.

Isaac dozes off in the passenger seat, wearing his plaid cap and a sweater to keep him warm against the air-conditioning.

I could play games or videos on my own phone, but I am trying to stay off the grid because I'm a meme. Somebody took a frame in my video reply to Cyrus and added the caption THAT'S NOT FUNNY. In that frame I look particularly red-faced.

I had a little sunburn from my camping trip, but nobody knows that, and nobody cares. I just look like I'm bawling. People have been posting the picture all over the internet, usually in response to anyone who says a joke is in bad taste. I've become the face of the easily offended, a crybaby who is triggered by anything. I may never go online again.

I've brought two books with me—*She's on the Case*, even though I've already read it, and a Ross Cooper book from the library—but reading in the car makes me feel carsick. So all I can do is be bored, think about things, and watch Wisconsin roll by.

Zach gets particularly worked up during one of the songs and bounces in the seat, crashing into me as he bops along with the music.

"Can you please stop it?" I ask him. But he can't hear, so I yank the headphones off his head.

"Hey!" He grabs them back, looking at me like I've punched him.

"Knock it off with the bouncing," I tell him.

"*You* knock it off."

"Knock what off? I'm not doing anything."

"Yes you are. You're being a Lucas," he says.

"What does *that* mean?"

"You know," he taunts. "It means you're a whiny little Zikito who doesn't want anybody to have any fun."

Zikito is a mosquito support character in *Smashtown*. He has a high-pitched buzz that summons a swarm of other Zikitoes who swirl around and annoy the enemy. He is probably the most despised character in the game.

"What did you call me?"

"You heard me." He puts his headphones back on, cranks up the volume, and bops along as violently as possible. I yank the headphones off again and call him something worse than a Zikito.

"Boys!" Yolanda barks. "If you can't get along, I'm going to leave both of you at the next rest stop."

"He started it," Zach mutters.

"I don't care who started it," Yolanda says. "I'm ending it."

I'm jealous of Isaac for being able to sleep through most of the seven-hour drive.

• • •

I try to get excited when I see the Chicago skyline six-plus hours later, but nervousness starts roiling in my stomach. The tournament will be hard. I am a meme. I've seen stories on the news about how Chicago has a lot of crime and slums. I imagine *Smashtown*-like alleyways infested by masked bandits. What if our hotel is in a slum?

Yolanda and Dad planned the trip together, booking a hotel suite north of downtown. It's close to where Isaac's mom lives and on a bus line so Zach and I can get to and from the tournament. Yolanda has GPS in her car and finds the hotel no problem. It is brick-red and on a street lined with trees. It's a cheap hotel but it's in a nice neighborhood.

There's a pizza place across the street.

"And all our meals are planned," Zach says, rubbing his

hands. "Chicago-style pizza is the best."

"What's the difference between Chicago pizza and regular pizza?" I ask.

"I don't know," he admits. "But I've *heard* it's the best."

We haul our bags up to the suite. There's a big room with a couch and two bedrooms. Yolanda and Isaac get the bedrooms. Zach and I get the living room. One of us will sleep on a rollaway cot and the other on the couch. Zach immediately grabs the remote and sprawls out on the couch. Isaac and Yolanda retreat to their rooms.

It seemed like a good idea at the time. I would have agreed to anything to get to the tournament. Spending three straight days with Zach seemed like a totally doable compromise.

But now I need a break from his watermelon-and-hot-Cheeto breath.

"I'm going to take a dip in the pool," I tell him, digging through my suitcase for my swimming trunks.

"Good idea," Zach says, flipping off the TV. "I could go for a swim."

"On the other hand," I say, "maybe I'll go later."

"OK." He flips the TV back on. He doesn't get the hint that what I really want is a break from him. I put on my swim trunks and flip-flops, hoping he'll get too caught up in the movie to follow. No such luck. He gets changed too, and since I'm already dressed for the pool, I let him follow me. I can't back out now without being totally rude.

We have the pool to ourselves. I splash around a bit. I'm not a great swimmer, but the cool water washes off the effects of the long drive.

"Aqua Tail!" Zach says, slicing his arm through the water to send a tsunami my way. I let it splash over me, then whirl around and send a small tidal wave back at him.

"Aqua Ring!" I announce. I haven't played a Pokémon game in a long time, but I remember all the moves.

"Hydro Pump!" he says, then takes a mouthful of water and sprays it at me.

"Dude! Not cool!" I wipe the spit-and-chlorine mix out of my face. Zach seems to take everything a notch higher than he should.

We both stop because a couple girls about our age in swimsuits have arrived. Pokémon is OK for two thirteen-year-old boys, but somehow not when girls are around. They kick off their flip-flops and drape towels over the chairs. There's something exotic about them just because they live in a different city. I mean, they don't live in *Chicago*, because they wouldn't be staying in a hotel, but they probably aren't from Minneapolis.

One of them looks at us, then whispers to the other. Then the other one looks at us and whispers back. They both giggle.

"Let's go make some friends," Zach says and starts walking through the water, using his arms as paddles. I follow. I usually don't walk up to strange girls, but we're in a city where nobody knows us. They don't have to know we were pretending to be Pokémon less than a minute ago.

"Hey," says Zach. "I'm Zach."

The girls trade nervous looks, then one of them answers.

"Hi. I'm Olivia and she's Sophie." Sophie smiles shyly at us. She is pale and freckled with short, light-brown hair and is wearing a red suit. Olivia has dark crinkly hair and light-brown skin and is wearing a sparkly blue bathing suit.

"I'm Lucas," I tell them.

"We're in Chicago for a tournament," Zach says. "What about you?"

"Ballet camp," Sophie says. "We're here all week." She slips into the water, takes a few freestyle strokes, stops and turns. Olivia follows her into the water and glides over beneath the surface. They're both so graceful. I feel short and pudgy and clumsy compared to them.

"So what sport do you play?" Olivia asks. The question seems out of the blue until I remember Zach mentioned a tournament, but not what kind.

"*Smashtown Frenzy,*" he says. "It's a video game. Do you play?"

"A little," Olivia says. "But not competitively. You must be good."

"Uh, yeah," he boasts. "We got first place in Minneapolis."

"Wow," she says.

"So, uh," Sophie finally speaks, "we have a question." She looks past Zach at me. Olivia shoots her a look, but Sophie plunges on. "Aren't you the 'that's not funny' guy?"

"Um . . ."

"He is!" Zach says.

"Wow!" she says. "You're famous!" Both girls giggle again. I couldn't turn a brighter red more quickly if I were dunked in paint. Now I match my meme.

"Which one do you think is cuter?" Zach asks as we make

our way back up to the room. We're supposed to go the pizza place with Yolanda and Isaac at six, and it's six now.

"They're both cute," I tell him. *And they're both graceful and gorgeous and way out of our league*, I think. It's not like Lia is *in* my league, but if I'm going to crush on a girl out of my league, her league can at least be in the same state as my league.

"I haven't decided which one I want yet," Zach says coolly.

I shake my head.

"What?"

"Dude, they're not candy bars in a vending machine," I tell him.

"I didn't say they were!"

"Besides, you probably won't see either one of them again. Even if you do, they live in Cleveland."

"They'll be here all week," he says.

"*We're* leaving the day after tomorrow. And we'll be kind of busy until then, if you haven't forgotten."

"You're jealous," he says after a moment.

"Of what?"

"Jealous that they like me. They think *you're* a Zikito. Because you *are* a Zikito. The whole world knows it." He adopts a high-pitched voice. "Strokes aren't funny!" As he says it, the elevator whooshes open and we see Yolanda and Isaac standing there, waiting for us.

"No, they are *not* funny," Yolanda says. She touches Isaac gently on the arm and gives us *both* a stern look, even though Zach is the one who said it.

We get dressed in a hurry and meet them at the pizza place.

Zach and I split a large pepperoni. Apparently the difference between Chicago pizza and everywhere-else pizza is the crust is really thick and there's too much sauce. The grown-ups get the salad bar.

Isaac picks quietly at his salad and doesn't say much. Every so often Yolanda shoots us a peeved look. She's annoyed that Zach made that crack about strokes, and probably thinks I was in on it. I want to tell her *I* wasn't in on it, but don't want to talk about it in front of Isaac.

It's been a long day, but not as long as tomorrow is going to be.

• • •

The next morning, I get dressed in brown shorts and a short-sleeved button-down shirt with green and white stripes. I also have new deck shoes and something called secret socks. The shoes are uncomfortable *without* socks, but you're not supposed to wear them *with* socks, so they make secret socks. Fashion can be dumb.

But I look sharp, I think. I complete the look with my new fishing cap.

When Zach sees me, he *tsks* in disapproval. "What's up with the uptight clothes, dude? Lia's not even here."

"What does Lia have to do with anything?" I ask innocently.

"Dude, she's in *high school*."

"She's only fourteen months older than me."

"She goes to *Bradley*." Bradley is a pricey private school where all the Sigh Borgs and KidsfromSLP go.

"So?" I say.

"So," he says, "you don't need to dress like *you* go to Bradley, because *A*, she already knows you go to public school—public *middle* school—and *B*, she's not even here."

"At least she lives in Minnesota," I tell him, thinking of the girls from the pool. He makes a *psh* noise, which is his way of admitting I've won the argument.

Meanwhile, Isaac is struggling to get his necktie right. They aren't leaving for hours, but he's already getting dressed. He's a lot more with it in the mornings, but he still hasn't got full use of his right hand, so it's hard.

I won't get to meet Maggie Ruth Biddle today, but the plan is for all of us to have breakfast tomorrow. If his mother wants to, that is.

"Your mother won't care if you wear a tie," I tell him.

"You don't know my mother," he says, finally getting the fat part of the tie to slide through the loop. He tightens the knot.

"You look good," I tell him.

We all head downstairs for the free breakfast buffet. Zach fills a plate with breakfast meat and doughnuts. I pour a ladle of batter into a waffle iron, flip it, and wait for it to ding.

"Good luck today!" A girl's cheerful voice rings through the lobby. I see Olivia and Sophie and a well-dressed woman—Olivia's mother, I guess—at one of the tables. All of them are eating fruit and yogurt.

"Thanks!" Zach hollers, waving at them with a piece of bacon. I want to add my own *thanks*, but I'm using a plastic fork to get my waffle unstuck from the iron.

Zach carries his breakfast over to the girls, but I sit down with Isaac and Yolanda. Isaac looks as nervous as I feel. He pokes at his eggs and doesn't eat much.

"Good luck with your mom," I say as I finish my waffles. I'm nervous too, but I love waffles.

"Good luck with your *Pac-Man Fever*," he says with a half-smile. I know he's having a good day if he can troll me a little with the *Pac-Man* stuff.

The tournament doesn't begin until noon, but we're supposed to be there by nine-thirty for a pre-tournament program: photo ops, some demos of new games, an early lunch with Streamcast stars, and other surprises. Zach and I are out the door at eight-thirty. The waffle settles into my gut like wet cement as we walk the two blocks to the bus station. I'm suddenly feeling anxious about everything—the tournament, finding my way through a big city, and being a meme. We buy our tickets from a machine, look at the map, and find the right curb to stand on. I planned out the bus ride before we even left, so I just need to make sure it's the right stop and the right bus and we're going in the right direction.

"Also, she's your sister," Zach says out of the blue.

"What?"

"You can't date Lia because she's your sister. Luke and Lia, get it?"

"Really? You've been working on a comeback for the last hour, and that's it?"

"It's funny," he says, cracking a corny grin.

"It's not the gag, it's the timing."

A bus comes along a bit later with the right number. *This is no harder than catching a bus in Minneapolis*, I think. We board the bus, slide our tickets into the box, and stand hanging on to the bars because the seats are full. But then I'm nervous about getting off at the right stop. When we do—I have to alert Zach, because he's playing on his phone—we find ourselves right out in front of the event center.

We did it!

Nobody notices me in the crowd as we enter, and that's another relief. Now all I have to be anxious about is the actual tournament.

We wait in the lobby for Noah and Max. They arrive with Max's parents and Tori, his dad looking around in wonder at the size of the crowd, the banners hanging from the high ceiling advertising the tournament, and the many merch tables selling stickers, T-shirts, and other *Smashtown* goodies.

"So this is really big, huh?" Max's dad says.

"That's what I've been trying to tell you!" Max says.

It is a big deal, I remind myself. *We were the best team in Minneapolis. We have a chance at being number one in the whole country.*

My private pep talk is interrupted when someone shouts "That's not funny!" at us. So much for total anonymity. I have my Cyrus fishing cap in my bag. I take it out and slam it on my head, pulling the long bill down to cover my face.

"Come on," Max says. "Let's check in." He hugs his parents and we all walk over.

We find the table for finalists to sign in. A white guy with dreadlocks is staffing the table, wearing a tie-dyed *Minecraft* T-shirt on which the Steve character *also* has dreadlocks. DREADBLOCKS, it says.

"You need to give us the credentials for the *Smashtown* account you'll be using," he tells us.

"Really?" Noah asks. "Why now?"

"To save time later," he explains. "The IT team will log you in for each match so you can sit down and battle. The first round is going to be pretty high speed."

"Cool," Noah says.

Max goes first, then Noah, then Zach. They each confirm their name and enter their usernames and passwords on a tablet that's chained to the table. When it's my turn I get an error message in beveled white letters against an angry red background.

ACCOUNT SUSPENDED.

"I must have typed something wrong," I say. "Can I try again?"

"Hmm." The guy turns the tablet around and spells out my username. "L-U-K-E-Z-I-L-L-A?"

"That's right," I tell him. "But maybe I entered my password wrong?"

"No," he says. "The error message says 'account suspended,' not 'password not recognized.'"

"But it's got to be a mistake!"

"Maybe, but I can't fix it. You'll have to contact customer support."

"Is there a customer support rep here?"

He shakes his head. "Not yet. Sorry dude. There's, like, a web form you fill out."

The life force drains from my body. Kogeki customer support is infamous for taking weeks to get back to you, if they do at all.

"But I'm in the tournament!" I hear the shrillness in my own voice. I'm living up to my meme. *This is not funny.*

"Not anymore," he says with a shrug. "You've been disqualified, mon."

CHAPTER 11

"But what about the rest of us?" Max protests. "*We're not suspended!*"

"Yeah," Noah asks. "The whole team isn't disqualified, is it?"

"Let me call someone." The guy gets on a phone and yaps for a while. He keeps his hand cradled around his mouth. I hope he'll find out there's been a mistake and wave me in. He finally gets off the phone.

"They say a team can replace up to one player if he or she can't participate for any reason," he says. "But unless you have someone here who can play with you—"

"We do! My sister!" Max's family is about twenty feet away, watching. Max waves at Tori to come over, then turns back to the guy in the Dreadblocks shirt. "My sister can play with us. It's actually her team!"

"What's going on?" Tori asks.

"You have to play with us," Max says. "Lucas can't play."

"Uh, sure." Tori looks stunned, apologetic, and thrilled all at the same time.

"She'll need proof of age and parental consent," says the guy at the table.

"Our parents are right over there! And she's already in your database because she played in Minneapolis." He waves his parents over.

"All right, then," Dreadblocks says. "Let's get you added to the roster."

"But . . . guys . . . ," I sputter.

"Sorry, Lucas," Max says. "I don't know what else to do." He puts a hand on my shoulder. "If it was me, I would want *you* to play."

"Um. Yeah. Of course I want you to play. Go on without me." I feel like the wounded guy in a war movie. The one who isn't supposed to survive.

Max's mom signs off on Tori playing in the tournament.

The guy in the Dreadblocks shirt hands Tori a tablet. She signs in, and the four of them have their bags checked, then disappear into the next room, Noah and Zach mumbling hasty apologies toward me. I'm left with Max's mom and dad, who look confounded and uncomfortable.

"So, we had plans," Mrs. Zeller says tentatively. "We were going to take in a couple sights before the tournament begins."

"If you want to join us, you're welcome to," Mr. Zeller adds. "We have an extra ticket to the Field Museum, because we had one for Tori."

"No thanks," I choke out. I walk away, my eyes blurring with tears. I look back once, wondering if they will come after me. Max's mom is on the phone, probably calling my mom.

I puzzle out what might have happened. I use the same login name for everything: Lukezilla. It's right there on my Streamcast page. Somebody guessed I used the same login name on *Smashtown*, hacked my account, and broke some rules to get me suspended?

If using those dedicated servers at Jacob's was the problem, we'd all be suspended, so that can't be it. Somebody had it in for me, personally.

I wonder if I can fix it. I can't open a ticket because I left my laptop in Minneapolis. We're not allowed to bring laptops into the competition, and I didn't want to leave mine in the hotel room all day. I could try to fill out the form on my phone, but typing a long explanation on a phone, trying to undo all the weird autocorrects, is more than I can manage when I'm shaking from rage and disappointment.

I could ask for someone in charge here, somebody to appeal to, make my case, see if they can let me in. But I no longer have a team. The 4LMNTs dropped me faster than a hot poker, as Cyrus would say.

• • •

I don't know what else to do, so I get on the bus to the hotel and slink to the back seats. My phone rings, and I grab at it, feeling a moment of hope. Maybe they figured things out and need me to come back? But no, it's Mom.

"Hi," I say, trying to sound normal.

"Max's mother said something went wrong with your registration?" she says.

"You can say that." I explain as best I can. "Somebody must have hacked my account."

"Why would they do that?"

"Because people are jerks," I answer. Mom and Dad don't know about my meme. It hasn't leaked into the worlds of middle-age people who don't play video games or watch Streamcast.

"I'm so sorry," she says. "Are you all right?"

"Not really," I tell her. The bus squeals to my stop. "But don't worry. I won't jump off the Sears Tower."

"That's not funny," she says. I guess that phrase runs in the family.

"Sorry. Anyway, I'll survive this somehow."

I get off the bus and slouch back to the hotel. I take the stairs up instead of the elevator, to make myself even more miserable, and let myself into what I expect to be a dark and empty room.

But Isaac is in the armchair, his tie still perfectly straight.

"You haven't even left yet?" I ask.

He shakes his head. It's a dumb question, I guess.

"What happened to your competition?" he asks.

"They didn't let me in," I explain in a hoarse voice. "They said I was disqualified."

He sits up a little straighter. "How come?"

"They think . . ." I pause and take a breath. "They think

I cheated or something." The only reason people get their account suspended is cheating, after all.

"Did you?"

"Heck, no!"

"Well, what do they think you did?"

"I don't even know." I throw myself on the sofa bed, still unfolded from last night. I want it to fold up with me in it so I can disappear.

"I once flew to New York for a mystery writer's conference," Isaac says. "My publisher paid for the whole trip. It was quite a big deal. I wanted to meet all the famous authors. I expected to be treated like a rising star. Well, we booked that trip before the book came out and got all the bad reviews. It wasn't the big hurrah I'd hoped for. I wandered the conference floor, unable to talk to anyone. One woman saw me—she was a very famous writer. I was a big fan of hers. She grabbed my arm and said, 'There you are!,' and for a moment I thought she'd read my book and was thrilled to meet me. But she handed me an empty glass and asked for another."

"Another what?"

"Another drink. She thought I was the waiter." Isaac snorts. "There weren't a lot of black faces there except for the help, you see."

"I'm sorry," I tell him, feeling a pang of outrage on his behalf.

"And I'm sorry for you," he says. "I know how you feel."

"Your story is worse."

"I wasn't thrown out," he says with a shrug.

"No, but . . ." I try to explain why his story is worse. Yolanda comes out of her bedroom. She's dressed up too.

"I thought you left," she says.

"I came back early." I don't want to explain everything a third time.

"Well, we have to go," she says, nodding at Isaac. He climbs slowly out of his chair and walks toward the door, looking as nervous as I felt an hour or so ago. He stops as he gets to the doorway and turns back.

"Do you want to go with us?" he asks.

"Really?" I wonder if he feels sorry for me or if he wants me to go. "I thought I'd just meet her tomorrow, after you two have a chance to talk."

"I could use you there," he says. "Moral support."

I look to Yolanda, who shrugs.

"You can come if you want," she says. "Just bring a book."

"OK. Sure." It's better than staying in the room, thinking about the awesome time my friends are having—and that I *should* be having. I grab my backpack on the way out, which has a couple books in it, my phone charger, and some snacks.

We drive across the Chicago River and then zigzag along residential streets. Yolanda parks by a tall white concrete building that says FAIRVIEW HEIGHTS RESIDENTIAL LIVING FOR SENIORS.

"Don't residential and living kind of mean the same thing?" I ask as we get out of the car. I just want to say something to cut through the weirdness of the moment.

Isaac snorts a laugh. Yolanda rolls her eyes.

We enter the lobby and Yolanda signs in and talks to a woman at the desk. Then Yolanda turns back to us and says, "You two wait in the lounge. I'll talk to her for a few minutes, then I'll bring her down."

Isaac nods. He looks like he's rethinking the whole idea of visiting his mother. He and I plop down in stiff chairs in the sunny lounge. He examines the leaves of a potted tree. I finger through something called *AARP* magazine, which is apparently for old people. The articles are all about health, saving money, and profiles of celebrities.

A few residents are sitting around, reading or chatting. Two of them are solving a crossword together, passing the folded newspaper back and forth. It's quiet and calm. We're not that far from the event center, but it feels like we're on another planet.

The time crawls. At long last, an elevator dings and Yolanda returns, pushing a wheelchair carrying a very old woman with a white knit shawl draped over her shoulders. Margaret Ruth Biddle fixes Isaac with a steely gaze. He slowly gets up from his chair to meet her.

"I didn't know if I'd ever see you again," she says.

"I'm sorry I didn't come sooner," Isaac says in a low voice, not making eye contact. "I didn't know if you wanted to see me."

"Hmph," Ms. Biddle says, drawing herself up in her chair. "Of course I want to see you. Who's the boy?" She notices me for the first time.

"Lucas is a neighbor of Isaac's, and a friend," Yolanda says. "He and his father are the ones who called the ambulance for Isaac."

"Did you come all the way to Chicago to meet me?"

"No, ma'am, I have—I had—I was coming to Chicago on other business." I almost never say things like "No, ma'am," and I've certainly never said "I came here on other business," but I'm trying to sound grown up.

"Well, thanks for helping my son," she says at last.

"Of course," I tell her. "I mean, you're welcome."

There's a long silence, so once again I try to fill it. "I've read about you. You really had an amazing life."

"*Had?*" she echoes. "Do you notice I'm still here?"

"I mean *have* an amazing life," I correct myself.

She smiles for the first time, and I know she's teasing me.

"Well, it is fair to say that the amazing part is over," she says. "I did try to leave my mark on the world." She looks to Isaac. "So why have you been too busy to come see your mother?"

He gulps.

"You didn't write! You didn't call!" she continues.

Yolanda looks like she wants to intervene but doesn't know what to say. I worry that it's up to me to help.

"I didn't think you wanted to hear from me," Isaac says at last.

"Hmph," she says again. "Of course I wanted to hear from my only son."

"He thought you were mad at him," I say timidly. I am

supposed to be moral support, after all. "Because of the book."

Ms. Biddle fixes me with her laser eyes.

"I'd forgotten all about his *mystery novel*," she says. She says *mystery novel* the same way my parents say *video game*.

"I thought it was great," I tell her. Everyone is looking at me, and every look is telling me to shut up, but I can't seem to stop myself. "I know you think Billie Ruth is an insult, because she's kind of over the top, but I think—I *know* Isaac meant it as a compliment. If the character seems like . . . an exaggeration, it's because that's how he sees you. Like a superhero."

Ms. Biddle looks like she's got her thumb on the dial to change her laser eyes from "smolder" to "atomize."

"Well, thank you so much for explaining it to me," she says. "Since I only have three college degrees I must need a lowbrow book explained to me. By a child."

"Sorry," I tell her. "I didn't mean it that way."

"Lucas, maybe I should drive you back to the hotel," Yolanda suggests gently but firmly. "That'll give Isaac and his mother a chance to catch up."

I get it. I've offended Isaac's mom, and she needs to be in a better mood so Isaac can make up with her.

"I saw a bus stop outside," I tell her.

"Are you sure you can find your way?"

I hold up my phone. "I can figure it out."

• • •

I have an app on my phone for Chicago Transit, and use it to figure out how to get back to the hotel. Just my luck—

the app tells me to hop on a bus and then transfer at the convention center.

As I ride, I wonder how Isaac's mother can be so hard on him, even after all these years. I know she had a hard life, but it seems after all this time she'd see that he's a good man even if he was never a hotshot lawyer. Plus, *she* could have called *him*.

The bus rolls up to the convention center and I hop off. The tournament will be starting soon. A couple hours ago, I would have thought I couldn't go in a million years, but now I think it'll be sadder all alone in my hotel room. I can transfer for up to two hours, so I decide to at least walk in and check things out.

This morning the place was busy, but now it's an absolute mob—a steady flood of people, mostly young, pouring through the atrium, thronging around the various tables, and going into the auditorium. I feel a wave of nervous excitement even though I'm not in the tournament. I put on my Cyrus cap and pull the bill down to hide my face, then go stand in line.

"Ticket?" the usher asks when I get to the door.

"I need a ticket?"

"Yes. The tickets were free, but you had to order them online." He squints at me. "Hey, I know you. You're the 'that's not funny!' kid."

"You got the wrong guy," I say in a small voice.

"Sure I do. Well, the event is sold out, so if you don't have a ticket . . ."

"I can't get in?" I say in disbelief.

"You can watch online. It's streaming."

"I don't have a computer with me."

The guy waves his hand down the hall. "They'll have it on in the overflow room. You don't need a ticket for that."

"OK, thanks." I leave the line and walk down the hall, not believing I came all the way to Chicago to watch the tourney on a *screen*. I could have done that at home.

The overflow room is huge, with a big screen in front and about two hundred chairs. In the back are some tables, with reporters typing on laptops and wearing lanyards with ID cards that say PRESS. I pull the bill of my cap even lower, and slump down in a seat. As I do, a nosy guy a couple seats over notices me and cranks his head to get a better look. I look straight ahead and pretend I don't notice.

The screen shows the stage with gaming tables and the screens behind them. A few technical people are walking around, checking cables, and tapping on microphones. You can see the first few packed rows of restless spectators on the lowest part of the screen.

The nosy guy aims his cell phone at me to snap a picture, doing it from a weird angle so I won't notice. I notice. I see him composing a message to post the photo online. This is the worst moment of my life. I'm all alone in a big city. I'm out of the tournament and thrown off my team. But I'm not even invisible, the way I am at school. I'm painfully visible.

I want to text Max or Noah or even Zach to find out what's going behind the scenes, but I also know they have to have their phones turned off while in the tournament room.

I do text Yolanda, because I want to text somebody, and Isaac doesn't use a cell phone.

Made it OK. Hope Isaac & his mom are getting along.

She responds with, *Glad you're good. It's awkward but they're talking.*

On the screen, I see the people in the first rows cranking their heads, looking at something off to the side. A moment later Cyrus Popp trots up the steps to the stage.

"Hello, Cyborgs!" he booms. The audience cheers. He begins by thanking a bunch of sponsors and partners, then gets to the point.

"We've been to thirty-two cities across the country. We've seen more than sixteen thousand teams compete and found the best-of-the-best *Smashtown* battle squads. There are still more than one hundred teams in competition for the title. But in the next two hours, they'll be winnowed faster than field mice in mowing season." He explains that there will be four matches running simultaneously. Every match is an elimination match.

At the end of his speech, he pumps the air with his hands to get the crowd going. But he *doesn't* "stroke out." In fact, the crowd seems to be waiting for it, and when it doesn't happen, there's a hiss like the air leaking out of a bouncy castle. Cyrus never replied to my video, directly or indirectly, but the non-use of the stroke routine feels like an answer.

Maybe it wasn't for nothing, I think.

Cyrus! Why hadn't I thought of him? He could help me.

This is his tournament, and if he tells Mr. Dreadblocks to let me in, Mr. Dreadblocks will say "Yes, mon!"

Then I remember I can't even get into the auditorium, let alone get to Cyrus.

I also remember that I don't have a team anymore. I've been replaced.

While I'm thinking things through, feeling a rush of hope and then the drain of reality, Cyrus is reading the names of the first eight teams. The KidsfromSLP are in the first set, but not the 4LMNTs. I watch anxiously, trying to keep track of their match while the screen cuts between their match and several others.

The Kids have stopped goofing around with lineups and have settled on what I know is their favorite set. Vile the snake (Jacob), Caprina the Ram (Emily), Honeypie the bee (Chloe), and good ol' Pango the pangolin (Nash). In the final match of the Minneapolis tournament, I took it as an insult, but now I know they went safe-and-comfortable for the last round. They weren't trying to show us up after all.

I watch for those characters. I haven't seen a *Smashtown* tourney as a spectator before, but I'm impressed by whoever's job it is to see all those screens—four matches, each with two teams, each team with four players—and instantly feed up the one with game-deciding action on it.

The KidsfromSLP win, and I can't help but shout and pump my fists in the air.

"We're friends," I hastily explain, looking at the floor so nobody—

LUKEZILLA BEATS THE GAME

"That's not funny!" somebody shouts.

—recognizes me. Too late. I slouch back in my chair while a few more people snap photos. The big screen shows the KidsfromSLP as they walk offstage, trying to keep their game faces on. But I can see that Jacob looks funny, pale and wobbling a bit. His eyes grow wide. He rushes toward the stage steps, holding up his hands to stop the . . .

You don't want to know.

. . .

But I have to tell you anyway.

Jacob, Mr. Cool and Laid Back Who Pretends He Doesn't Care, throws up on the stage.

He tosses his cookies.

He loses his lunch.

He ejects matter from his stomach through his mouth, as the dictionary explains.

He mouth-poops, as I called it at age three in a story my parents love to tell.

And he does it on a *nationally streamed live video watched by millions.* Because the same techies I was admiring for finding the best action on screen also find it onstage.

I do feel sorry for him, but I also think, *that ought to knock 'That's not funny' off the leaderboard.* Which I immediately feel guilty about.

To feel better about the guilt, I tell myself he'll be fine. He goes to Bradley. His dad is not only rich enough to buy a house on Lake Minnetonka and have his own foosball table, he has special access to the *Smashtown* servers.

Then I feel bad again, not because Jacob is embarrassed, but because he's sick. It would suck to be sick on the day of the tournament.

In both the auditorium and the overflow room, people are wincing in disgust, covering their own mouths, and/or laughing in sudden donkeylike brays. And when that dies down, I feel hundreds of eyes turning to me, because I have announced that Pukey McVomitbreath is my pal.

"Poor guy," I announce, looking at the floor. I sit down and pull the bill of my hat even farther down. At this point I could tuck it into my collar. People lose interest and look back to the screen.

Over the hubbub you can faintly hear Cyrus's voice calling the names of the next teams to play at that table, and he names the 4LMNTs. Max, Noah, Tori, and Zach hurry up to the stage. It's a gut punch to see them without me, but today has been the loneliest of my life, so it's also good to see familiar faces. They get into position as their opponents take their seats across from them—four guys from Mississippi who won the New Orleans tournament. Their team name is Tupeloxi.

"Two teams from opposite ends of the Mississippi River," Cyrus says.

I find myself rooting for the 4LMNTs in spite of my hard feelings. It's not their fault that I got hacked.

The 4LMNTs have a new lineup with Spry, Spike, Pirrot, and Pango. Tupeloxi has Krawk, Crusher, Kathulopter, and Isborg. Which means Tupeloxi chose size and toughness

LUKEZILLA BEATS THE GAME

over speed and agility, which our team—oops, I mean, the
4LMNTs—are good at countering. Max is really good with
Spry. I've honestly seen nobody in either tournament with his
reflexes and dead-on accuracy. As the game gets started, I see
that Max is at his best now, even though he hasn't played with
Spry in a while. He torments the hyena and polar bear and
skips away without taking damage, using their big bodies to
shield himself from the squid's inky blasts and the crocodile's
devastating bite. Pirrot follows his motions so perfectly it's
like one player is controlling both characters with the same
keyboard. She boosts his health up whenever he does take a
little damage. I feel my pulse pound and realize I'm as wound
up *watching* my old team as I get playing with them.

The match goes on forever, but the 4LMNTs grind it out
and take down their opponents' wall.

"Wow!" Cyrus says as the Mississippi team shuffles off
the stage. "Remember, Tupeloxi beat out more than eight
hundred teams in New Orleans, but the Minneapolis team
packed their lunch pail and sent them to school!" I hear faint
booing from the crowd, probably because the 4LMNTs still
have some haters, but a swell of cheering drowns them out.
There was nothing lucky or fixed about that match.

"That's not funny!" someone calls to the 4LMNTs as the
cheering dies out, followed by a smattering of applause and
laughter. Can't they see I'm not even there?

A heavy hand falls on my shoulder. I peer up and see a
huge guy looming over me, a laminated card dangling from a
lanyard. The card has one big, bold word: SECURITY.

"Lucas Sabbatini?" he says.

"Yeah." I feel like the endless series of bad luck won't stop. "Am I in trouble for being here? The ticket-taker guy told me it was all right."

"Cyrus wants to see you," the guard says. "Come with me."

CHAPTER 12

The security guy leads me back toward the auditorium.

"How'd you know where I was?" I asked him.

"Some guy posted a picture on Instagram and hashtagged it. So Cyrus asked me to fetch you."

"Oh right." I'm famous. At least my face is famous.

"If you have a computer in that bag you have to check it. And turn off your phone while you're in the auditorium."

"I don't have my laptop." I shut off the phone. As we pass the security guy at the auditorium door, the guard with me nods at him and he lets us both in.

The auditorium has screens I couldn't see from the other room, one for every match, all around the room. Pulsing techno music is playing loud enough to make the air vibrate. It is total sensory overload, but I'm glad because we can walk up the side aisle without anyone noticing me.

Almost anyone, that is, because I see Tori in the cordoned-off area for competitors, swiveling her head as we walk toward the stage. She looks shocked—eyes and mouth wide open.

What's going on? her look seems to ask.

I don't know either, I signal with a quick shrug.

I see worry in her eyes. If I'm allowed back into the competition, she knows the most likely scenario is she'll be off the team. But would they let me back in at this point, now that they've already played their first round? I shouldn't get my hopes up.

We head up a set of stairs and through a curtain backstage.

"Wait here," the guy says. There are a few folding chairs and a card table covered with snacks and bottles of water. I don't know if I'm allowed to sample the snacks, but they remind me that I haven't eaten since breakfast. I'd been too busy, nervous, and upset to think about food.

I awkwardly pull my backpack around to my front, unzip it, and grope around for a granola bar. As I do, somebody bumps into me from behind and sends the stuff in my backpack spilling out on the floor.

"I'm sorry!" a middle-age woman says. She crouches to help me gather my things.

"It's all right," I assure her, wondering who she is. Most of the people running the show here are young and male. "Are you Cyrus Popp's mom?"

She laughs. "No, I'm his boss."

"Cyrus Popp has a boss?"

"I'm the closest thing to it," she says. "I'm an executive producer with Streamcast and I'm the one running this show. My name is Cheryl."

"I'm Lucas," I tell her.

"Oh, I know who you are," she says. "Your fame precedes you. 'That's not funny?'"

I gulp, then nod.

"And for the record, I agree with you one hundred percent. I'd been trying to get Cyrus to drop that routine for the tournament. What he does on his own show isn't my problem, but the tournament has sponsors and we don't need bad P.R. Anyway, it's insulting and unnecessary, so thank you." She drops a bag of Fritos in my backpack, then folds up a sweatshirt and pushes it on top, crushing the chips. She starts to put the book in but stops to glance at the cover.

"*She's on the Case?*" She flips it over and looks at the back. "Interesting reading for a kid your age. Shouldn't you be reading *Harry Potter?*"

"I've read those too," I tell her. "But this is a good one, if you like mysteries."

"I love mysteries. In fact, I've been looking for one to read on the flight to England." She checks the inside flap and quietly reads the summary. "This sounds interesting."

"Do you want to borrow it?" I ask.

"Really?"

"Sure. I've already read it. You can mail it to me when you're done."

"Thanks, Lucas." She tucks it into her purse after I write my name and address on the inside back cover.

"*There* you are," says Cyrus, walking in from the stage. "Lukezilla. The boy who memed."

"I didn't mean to," I say.

"The internet," Cyrus says, flinging his hands up in a helpless gesture. "It's nuttier than a squirrel turd." He grabs one of the bottles, twists off the cap, and takes a drink. "I saw you were in the overflow room so I sent someone to fetch you. You should not be in exile. For the record, I don't think you cheated."

"I didn't," I tell him. So maybe I really am getting back in?

"I can't do anything about that," he says, quickly crushing my hopes. "I don't work for Kogeki Games. But listen. You do have fans. You could build on it. Make something of it."

"How do you mean?"

"People are paying attention. If you want to be a Streamcaster, this is your chance. Post a new video every day saying something isn't funny? Maybe not that, but milk it. Grow your platform." He gestures at Cheryl with his water bottle. "She'll tell you. You don't have to appeal to everyone on Streamcast. You just have to find the people who like what you're dishing out."

"It's true," she says. "It's the big difference between us and broadcast media."

"Uh, OK." He had somebody pull me from another room to tell me that? "I would love to be a Streamcast star."

"It's not as easy as people think," Cyrus says, "but it's better than working at the garden center at Walmart. Which is what I did before."

"I knew that. I've read all about you. I want to be like you when I grow up."

"Don't be like me," he says. "Be like Lucas. I'm taken."

I nod. I get what he means.

"So I wonder if you'd want to start here?" Cyrus says. "Make an appearance. Surprise people with a cameo. Like, listen. What if I start to stroke—"

Cheryl shakes her head so furiously it's like she has spiders in her hair. Cyrus stops.

"OK, not that. But to make the most of it, you should come out and yell *'that's not funny!'* The crowd will love it."

"What's not funny?"

"I don't know," he says. "It can be anything."

"Nothing that'll get us in trouble with an outspoken community that will threaten to boycott our sponsors," Cheryl quickly adds.

"Which means, almost anything that's actually funny," says Cyrus. He snaps his fingers. "Did you see that kid hurl on the stage? I'll say 'I'm so excited, I'm going to chuck my chowder!'"

"Gross," Cheryl says, but then laughs and holds her thumb up in approval.

"He's a friend of mine," I tell them.

"Even better," Cyrus says, "Listen, the best way for you to turn this around is to show that you have a sense of humor." He throws an arm around my shoulders. Cyrus Popp, palling it up with me. I can't believe it.

"You want me to walk out and shout, 'That's not funny!'"

"Yes," says Cyrus. "Say it like you mean it and stamp your foot. I think you'll be a big hit."

"If you're comfortable with it," Cheryl says cautiously.

"Of course he's comfortable with it," says Cyrus. "Because

the internet is wrong about Lukezilla. He has a great sense of humor, right?"

"Sure," I say uneasily. "I mean, when stuff is funny." *And puking is funny,* I tell myself. It's not the same as stroking out, because everybody throws up.

"So come on, man! Let's do this and make Streamcast history!"

I can't seem to say yes, but I can't seem to say no either. For a long time I stand there, both of them looking at me.

"Cyrus, it was worth a shot," says Cheryl, "but let's not push him. He clearly isn't comfortable with it."

"You don't think puking is funny?" Cyrus asks me.

"I do," I tell him. "It would be funny. But I . . . don't want to do it."

"He has stage fright," Cheryl says sympathetically. But she's wrong. That's not it. I feel like I'd be betraying . . . not Jacob, but Isaac. By making a joke out of the first video. Which, it occurs to me, Isaac doesn't even know about.

"Well, I have to get back out there." Cyrus turns around and trots out to the stage without a goodbye.

"Thanks for considering," Cheryl tells me.

"Um . . . can I ask for one small favor?"

"Sure."

"I want to stay and watch the tournament, so I can root for my friends, but I don't have a ticket."

"Of course," she says.

She finds a lanyard on the table and hands it to me. It's got the Streamcast logo on it and says CREW. "There are seats that say 'reserved for Streamcast.' Help yourself to any of those. Enjoy the tournament!"

• • •

I am an idiot, I think as I walk to the seats she mentioned, which are unfortunately in the center section, so I have to walk by every team in the tournament. In this tournament the losers stay with the winners, the two groups mixed up like there's no difference between them. Once again Tori gives me a frightened, curious look. Once again, I shrug. I do know what's going on, but how can I say 'They wanted me to do a bit on stage with my hero, but I said no because I'm an idiot' with body language? I drop down into one of the empty seats, drawing curious looks from nearby Streamcast staffers. I show them the tag dangling from my lanyard. One of them gives me a little nod, which I think means he recognizes me.

"We've culled the herd," Cyrus says dramatically. "We've separated the wheat from the chaff. We've boiled down the mash. But now it's time to raise the heat." He pauses, maybe trying to think of another metaphor.

I feel a hand on my arm and expect a security guard. But it's Nash, one of the KidsfromSLP. He gestures with his head to go with him so we can talk.

As we make our way up the aisle, Cyrus says the competition is tighter than a Speedo on a Sasquatch. Nash and I ease out the door and into the lobby.

"What?" I ask crossly. Nash has never been especially nice to me, so I'm not feeling especially nice back.

"Can you play for Jacob?" he asks. "We're still in the tournament, but he's really sick."

"I know, I saw," I tell him. "I can't play because my account is suspended."

"Yeah, everybody's talking about that," he says hastily. "But it's *your* account that's suspended. You would have to use *Jacob's* account to play with us. Because they log us in automatically, remember? All you'd do is sit down and play."

"They'll see me go up there," I tell him. "And everybody knows who I am." I'm not flexing my fame, it's simply true.

"They said we could find a substitute," Nash tells me. "They didn't say he couldn't be you. In fact, it's good that it's you, because they already have you registered. They have your proof of age and permission from your parents."

"I'm not exactly popular, in case you didn't notice."

"We don't have a lot of options," Nash admits. "And besides, you are a heck of a noob Smasher, Lucas. And we've played together, we know each other's moves. That's important."

"Yeah," I agree. "If they let me play, can I be Trunkzilla?"

"Whatever you want," he says. "I'm usually the tank, but I can take the assassin role."

"Then I'll do it. I mean, if they let me."

"Come on," he says. "Let's get this sorted out. The next round begins any minute."

• • •

"Sabbatini . . ." A guy at the registration table taps on his tablet, then shakes his head. "Not in here."

"Two *bs*," I tell him. I've already spelled it for him, but people can't seem to get it straight on the first try. I've heard Dad go through this a million times on the phone.

"That's what I have," he says.

"It ends in T-I-N-I," I tell him.

"Ah, I had Sabba-taaah-ni, it's Sabba-teeeh-ni." He taps some more. "Looks like you're all clear. We have proof of age and parental permission."

"My *Smashtown* account was suspended," I tell him. I want to make sure they know. I don't want my new team to win only to have the victory taken away if they discover my account issue later. "I didn't do anything, though. I think somebody hacked my account."

"Have you contacted Kogeki support?"

"No. I haven't had a chance. I just found out this morning that it was suspended."

"Hmm. Hey, Elaine?"

A young woman comes over; she's wearing a badge with the Kogeki logo on it. "Oh hey, it's you," she says, recognizing me from the meme.

"Can this kid play in the tournament if his *Smashtown* account is suspended?"

"I didn't actually do anything," I add.

"There is an appeals process," she tells me. "You have to go to tech support, open a ticket, and give your side of the story."

"I know all that, but that'll take days. The match is *right now*."

"Hmm. Well, if you're not playing on the same account

there's nothing stopping you." She looks thoughtful. "Let him play," she tells the guy in a low voice but loud enough for us to hear. "His account was probably breached. It's got hacker prints all over it."

"Thanks!" I say, even though she's not officially talking to me. *Where was she this morning?* I wonder.

"Looks like you can play," the guy says. "Good luck to you."

CHAPTER 13

As soon as we get to our seats, we hear the KidsfromSLP called for the second round. There is a clamor of mutters, boos, and complaints when people notice me.

"Cheater!" one voice bellows above the noise.

"He's been cleared for takeoff," Cyrus assures the crowd. "Come on, you all know one of you hooligans hacked the kid. And *that's not funny!*"

A smattering of laughter ripples through the crowd.

Never mind the haters. I get to play, and I get to be Trunky.

Our opponents are about my age, four girls, including one who uses a wheelchair. They're name is Dracarys. They wear matching pink T-shirts with a picture of a dragon.

"Hey," I nod at them. It's good to see another young team in the tourney. But if they've come this far, they're going to be tough to beat.

The match is set in Bush Boulevard, one my favorite arenas. It's a wide street made into a maze by crushed cars and crumbled buildings, which suits Trunky fine. He can stomp over rubble that slows down other characters. Being Trunky on Bush Boulevard is like coming home after a long, terrible day.

I lead the way through the refuse, letting my big elephant body shield Vile as he slithers after me.

They have two assassins, Krawk and Zigzap, and no cannon. Zigzap the eel works as a cannon for range attacks, but he's not effective at bringing down a fortress wall. Their tank is Tortuga, and they also have Kathulopter squidding around and inking things up. Their characters are big and slow, but this is a good arena for them.

Vile makes a stab at Krawk and is zapped by the eel.

He steals back to heal, and Honeypie lets loose with a honey bomb to buy time. Now we're frozen in the middle of the map. The opponents' characters are stuck in the honey, but our characters have trouble getting around them.

I nervously drum my thumb to the left of the keys, waiting, waiting. The second the honey-stick disappears, I lay down a stomp and freeze them a moment longer. Vile springs at the right time and hits the Krawk. Caprina surges forward, catching their tank with her horns.

The whole fight is a brawl, bodies crashing into bodies, but we make slow progress down the map, pushing and shoving through ink and honey until we press them against their own fortress wall. Caprina rams the wall and Trunky stomps through the rubble to reach their base.

"Woohoo!" I punch the air with my fists. Lots of people celebrate when they win, but of course I get booed for it, because I'm me.

"Good game," I tell the four girls.

"Yeah, it was," says the girl in the chair. "By the way, I liked your video. Seriously."

"Oh. Thanks." The boos continue.

"I guess you were serious about the haters," Nash whispers.

"Yep," I tell him.

"But I'm feeling good about our chances," he says. He slaps my shoulder as we sit down.

I'm sitting on the aisle, and the girl from the last round wheels up next to me.

"You've been re-memed," she says, showing me her phone.

"We're not supposed to have our phones on," I remind her.

"What are they going to do? Kick me out? I'm already out."

"Oh right." I glance at the phone. I don't want to be seen with it in case *I* get in trouble. There's a screen cap of me celebrating the victory—hands in the air, mouth open, face sweaty and shiny in the bright light. It's not exactly my best look.

Now THAT'S FUNNY, the caption says.

"Do you like it?" she asks.

"Sure. I guess I deserve it," I tell her.

"Good. I made it," she admits. She turns off the phone and puts it back in her bag.

"Sorry. I didn't mean to be a jerk."

"Oh, you were fine," she says. "I would have done the same thing."

I find out her name is Gabby, short for Gabrielle. She's from Delaware, and her team made the final four in Philadelphia.

165

"But we were completely trounced by PupSouth in the quarterfinals," she says.

"PupSouth?"

"Those guys," she gestures toward a group of boys in hoodies kicking back in their seats.

"Oh, I remember them." I'd watched the Cyrus Popp recap. "They act all . . . tough."

"They do," she nods. "But I hear they're really from Lower Merion." She rolls her eyes. "It's a really nice suburb," she explains when she sees the blank look on my face. "Anyway, they are scary good."

I glance up at the stage and see the 4LMNTs crushing somebody.

"They're good too," she says.

"Yeah, I know." I decide not to tell her they're my old team.

"The Spry and the Pirrot are so tight," she says in admiration.

"Yep." She can't know every word is a twist of the knife. At least I get to play now.

● ● ●

We watch a handful of matches, then another. Sixty-four teams become thirty-two. Like field mice in mowing season, as Cyrus said.

Next round, the KidsfromSLP take out a team from Houston called Xalting. Xalting starts strong but falls apart, arguing with each other after their Squunk backfires on their own Gurrilla. Our team has fallen into a rhythm—Trunky stomping ahead, Vile snaking around his legs and dealing damage, Honeypie laying down the stick, and Caprina speeding by and hammering the wall.

"Sixteen *thousand* teams competed nationwide," Cyrus tells the crowd. "And now it's down to just sixteen. These remaining teams are literally one in a thousand."

We find ourselves trotting up to the stage at the same time as the 4LMNTs for the round. We're not playing each other, but at the same time, at adjacent tables. Max and Tori look shocked. Noah shrugs. Zach waves. There's no time for me to explain or them to ask questions. "Good luck," I tell them over the buzz of noise. They're playing PupSouth, the "tough guys" from the streets of the affluent suburbs of Philadelphia. It's time to play my own match, so I try to forget about my old team.

We're playing 5Kdollar, the first-place team from the Phoenix tournament.

The arena is Grimway Grotto, a partially collapsed bridge full of potholes and fallen beams. It's a tough arena for Trunky, easier for the jumpers and climbers.

They front with Fumungus, belching smoke and fire, the big polar bear Isborg, my old friend Mustina, and Bizzard at support. Bizzard shortens your respawn time, which means—

"They want quick, ugly battles," I whisper into my mic.

"We know," Emily's voice rings over my headset. "If only we had a tank to stop them."

I'm Trunky, of course. Emily is Caprina the ram, Chloe is Honeypie the bee, and Nash is Vile the snake.

I keep Trunky back and protect the wall while Honeypie slows their charge. Vile and Caprina skirt either side, using their speed to avoid the fiery salamander. If they want quick, violent battles, we'll give them a long, drawn-out game of tag.

And because the match is long and drawn-out, and my only role is to stand and wait, I steal a glance at the projection screen showing the 4LMNTs' match and see Spike charging at an enemy wall. I wonder if it's Noah's Spike.

"Uh, Lucas?" Emily's voice sounds urgent over my headset.

I look back to my monitor and see Mustina savaging my flank. I let down a stomp and Mustina sprints away. Trunky can take a lot of damage, but I can't make mistakes like that.

A swell of noise from the audience tells me something exciting is going on. Probably the 4LMNTs and PupSouth. I clench my teeth and resist the temptation to look.

Mustina attacks again, catching me only slightly off guard, but dealing more damage. I need to back off and heal, but that would leave the wall open for Fumungus, who is right behind the badger, shooting flames. I don't even know where the others are or what they're doing. I hit the tab key to see the full map for a moment. Caprina is at their wall but is strafing left and right, avoiding the polar bear. She's unable to get consecutive hits in the same spot. Vile is harassing Isborg, but his health meter is beeping red.

I tab back in the nick of time and lower the boom on the badger. She scampers away to health up, which gives me a chance to do the same.

The crowd loses its mind over something. Hoots and hollers, cries of astonishment, and a huge collective groan, followed by thunderous applause.

"Can you believe that?" Cyrus's voice shouts. "Can you believe that? The Minneapolis champs have not run out of miracles!"

I can't help but glance back, just for a second, to see the Lukezilla-less 4LMNTs trading high fives. When I turn back to the game, Fumungus spews a burst of flame, and Trunkzilla vanishes. The timer appears on my screen counting down thirty seconds to respawn. *So we're the latest mice in the mower,* I think as Fumungus blasts the wall. Honeypie drops a sticky bomb on the salamander to buy us a second of time. I tab to the map to see the whole arena. Caprina finally gets enough hits at their wall. It quakes and falls at the same time ours does. Vile slithers in and touches the base.

Both bases turn yellow.

You TIE, the screen says. Ties almost never happen in *Smashtown.* The timer is sensitive to hundredths of a second. Even when teams *try* to tie, it's hard to do.

"It's a TIE!" Cyrus says, dragging the word out in a dismal way. "It's like getting underwear for Christmas, isn't it? Which means an immediate death match with additional hazards. You have three minutes to fight. If time runs out without a victor, *both teams are eliminated.*"

The timer is already going for the do-over. 3 . . . 2 . . . 1 . . .

We all respawn at the starting places with full health. The potholes are wider and deeper, some of them spouting steam. The bases are still exposed and yellow, because now it's a death match.

"Go for broke," says Nash.

I run at the other tank, barely getting around the plumes of steam as I thunder across the map and barrel into the bear, trying a tusk attack I rarely use. Vile goes after the badger. Caprina runs horns-first into the salamander. Honeypie drops a defensive stick-bomb in front of our wall.

One by one the characters fizzle from the screen. First Mustina, then Isborg, then Vile as the snake takes a jet of flame from the salamander. Caprina finishes Fumungus, then dies herself. They might have time to respawn before time elapses with Bizzard's boost, but that won't help them win. They wouldn't have a chance to take Trunkzilla and Honeypie down. It would only help us lose.

I need to kill the buzzard. It's rare to take out a support character; they fly above the fray. Honeypie zooms after it, chasing it into a plume of smoke leftover from Fumungus's scorching. She then flies over and sprays honey. Bizzard zooms toward me. The respawn timer for Mustina is at 5 . . . 4 . . . 3 . . .

I catch the bird with my tusks and bring it down and stomp. The buzzard dies a second before the badger comes back, nine seconds before the end of the game.

You win!

The crowd goes bananas. I can hear the roar even before I rip off the headset.

I look at the kids from Phoenix, wondering which one was the buzzard. They are all wearing stone-cold poker faces.

"Good game," I tell them, but they don't return the compliment. I don't think they mean to be rude. They're stunned by the loss. "Thank you," I add in a low voice. One of them nods. The guy who played as the buzzard, I suspect.

"They let us win," Nash mutters as we head back to our seats. "Their Bizzard could have flown anywhere and run out the clock."

"They wouldn't have won, though," Chloe says. "Both teams would have been out."

"But they could have dragged us down with them," says Nash. "They *let* us win because they were going to lose anyway."

"It was cool of them," I say. I was already thinking the same thing. Why would the buzzard fly straight to me unless they wanted to give us a chance?

"Who cares how it happened? We're still alive!" Chloe says. "We survived a sudden death overtime!"

"Well, we wouldn't have had to go to OT if *somebody* had been paying attention to the team he's *on*," Emily says pointedly. She glares at me when she says *somebody*. "You almost lost the whole tournament for us, Lucas."

"He's the one who took out Bizzard!" Chloe protests. "If he hadn't done that, we *would* be out of the tournament. And we wouldn't be in the tournament at all if he hadn't been here to sub for Jacob."

We've reached our seats, but the argument rages on.

"Sure, lucky *us* that Lucas cheated and got kicked off his first team," says Emily.

"Oh, you know full well he didn't cheat," Chloe argues. "One of the haters hacked his account. *Nobody* thinks he actually cheated."

"But he brought that on himself by having no sense of humor," Nash piles on.

"Fine. Blame the victim!" Chloe says.

I'm staying out of it, even though they're arguing about me. I feel a touch on my arm. Gabby has leaned way over to get my attention, reaching across an empty seat from her chair in the aisle.

"Hey," she says. I move into the empty seat next to her.

"Hey."

"You almost blew it," she tells me.

"I know."

"But you didn't," she says. "So . . . way to go?"

"Thanks." Suddenly the full weight of the day hits me. The meme, the trip, being hacked and exiled and returned, meeting Cyrus again, disappointing him. Being on a team that doesn't want me, in front of a crowd that mostly doesn't like me. Isaac and his mother . . . I wonder if Yolanda sent an update, but we're barred from using phones during the tournament.

Gabby is peering at me, her face full of concern.

"Are you all right?"

I shrug. I don't know what *all right* means anymore.

"I guess so," I tell her.

Fortunately there's a break between rounds, enough time to pull myself together. I go to a water fountain to splash water on my face and get a drink. When I get back, all the tables have been hauled away but two, which are placed in a V-shape with all the laptops facing the audience.

"One match at a time now," I tell Gabby.

"And everyone in the spotlight," she says. "It's pretty exciting. I wish I had someone to root for." She gives me a sideways look.

"Hilarious," I reply.

I glance over at the 4LMNTs. Max and Tori and Noah all have game faces on, but Zach is talking excitedly. He notices me and makes the Cyrus Popp gesture, pointing his thumb sideways and turning it up. I do the same.

"The quarterfinals!" Cyrus exclaims. "The first up is an *epic* rematch of one of the road finals, with the epic twist of one player switching teams."

Please let there be two other teams that fit that description, I think. I'm not ready to play my own team.

"The 4LMNTs, and the KidsfromSLP!" Cyrus announces.

No such luck.

CHAPTER 14

The 4LMNTs hurry onto the stage with hand slaps and fist bumps, the crowd cheering. The KidsfromSLP lag behind, barely looking at each other.

Winning is the best revenge, I remember.

3 . . . 2 . . . 1 . . . BATTLE!

The arena is Harang Drive, a wide, pocked road with tall, ruined warehouse-style buildings on either side. There are secondary lanes that twist around the buildings, some areas requiring leaping and climbing. It occurs to me that Harang Drive looks a little like the road Isaac lives on.

I have Trunkzilla stomp up the middle lane, flanked by Nash's Vile and Emily's Caprina. Chloe's Honeypie soars on ahead to stick up the path in front of Max's Spry, who is swinging and scrambling down the side lane. As always, Tori's Pirrot hovers faithfully close by, ready to heal the squishy assassin as soon as he takes damage. Noah's Spike and Zach's Pango march up the middle lane, meeting us in the center of the arena.

Trunky stomps, Spike and Caprina charge, Vile hisses and slithers away. Spry evades Honeypie and hurdles over a fence to get behind us, punching and pinching and scurrying away. It's hard to fight facing both ways, but Vile spins around and chases the monkey back to the side, pinning him against the fence and sinking ferocious fangs into him. Honeypie gets herself tangled up with Pirrot so she can't help.

The audience groans as Spry fades from the screen. Max's monkey has been the star of the 4LMNTs all day.

Caprina and Trunkzilla chase their tank and cannon back to their wall. They stand stout, defending their base. But we can't give them time for Spry to return. Caprina charges right at Pango. He uses a roll maneuver to dodge, which is fine because Caprina rams the wall, backs up, and prepares to charge again.

I go head to head with the rhino, trading hits and slams. Trunky can win any one-on-one in the game because of his high health. I start to feel good about our chances. Spry will respawn before the match is over, but we've got a huge lead in cracking their wall and dealing damage to their other fighters.

Caprina takes another lunge at Pango. Pango dodges and Caprina crashes into a short run of fence, getting her horns caught. She mashes her head, trying to pull free. I realize with a sick feeling that she's been lured into a trap. Emily mutters a few bad words into our headphones.

"I'm sorry! I should have seen it coming."

Spry returns, swings down, and assaults Trunkzilla with a fury. Free of Caprina, Pango is able to do roll-dashes at me, and Spike gouges me with his horns as I try to sidestep. Vile is afraid to come to Trunkzilla's aid with all his stomping around, Honeypie can't help without hindering, and Caprina is still trying to wrench her horns free.

She finally gets free, but too late. Trunky is dead and all four 4LMNTs are charging at our wall. Honeypie lays down a stick bomb but they veer around it. Spike and Pango take turns at the wall. Spike charges and Pango roll-dashes until they bring it crumbling down.

Trunkzilla respawns and takes a stance in front of the base, but Pirrot simply circles around and dives on the base.

You Lose!

The words flash red across the screen, then fizzle out like my hopes and dreams.

"Good game," Max says first, echoed by the others.

"Yeah. Good game," I manage to croak to my old pals. It was, for them. They outplayed us. They outfought, outmaneuvered, and outwitted us at every turn.

The 4LMNTs get a roar of audience approval as they walk triumphantly back to their seats. Apparently they've won over all the skeptics who thought the tourney was fixed.

The KidsfromSLP follow slowly, and we take our seats. Gabby gives me a sympathetic look.

"At least you got to play?" she says when the noise of the crowd finally dies down.

"Yeah. At least that."

• • •

That wave of victory carries the 4LMNTs all the way through the championship. I cheer them on. It's hard, but they are my friends, and they beat us fair and square. They did ditch me, but it wasn't their fault someone hacked my account.

It starts to feel like a game again, instead of the most important thing in the world. I realize Gabby is right. At least I got to play. This is way better than sitting back at the hotel, trying to watch the match on my phone.

The last match is a good one too, but the 4LMNTs pull it off. I find myself standing up and hollering and clapping with everyone else as the four of them wave to the crowd, beaming.

As the applause goes down, the lights dim. Every screen starts to play the trailer for *Smashtown Fury*, the same one we've seen already. The crowd cheers as loudly as if Lil Nas X has ridden his horse onto the stage singing "Old Town Road."

There are new words at the end:

WATCH WORLD PREMIERE LIVE GAME PLAY STREAM WITH CYRUS POPP

STARTS: FRIDAY, AUGUST 24, 7 P.M. EST

ENDS: ????

"That's right, Cyborgs!" Cyrus shouts into the microphone. "And guess what? Everyone in the competition gets exclusive access three days early. Maybe I'll see some of you in the game!"

The crowd reaches a new peak of loudness. I get excited myself, then remember I won't be able to play—my own account is suspended, and I played with Jacob's account all day today.

The lights go back on and Cyrus hands out trophies; bigger,

fancier versions of the ones we got in Minneapolis. They don't give them out for eighth place, so I don't get one. The applause is thunderous for the 4LMNTs. I cheer too, even though I'm really jealous. Who knows? Maybe with me instead of Tori they wouldn't have won.

After the awards, the champions—aka my former teammates—are surrounded by a small crowd of reporters. One of the Chicago newspapers is there, and a cable sports network, but mostly its gaming mags and websites. The 4LMNTs let Tori do most of the talking, as the oldest member and founder. She's also the only one who isn't too stunned to talk.

"It seems like you dominated the competition throughout the day. Was there a point where you felt like this could slip away from you?" one journalist asks.

"The team from Philadelphia—PupSouth," Tori says. "That's the best team we faced all day." In the background I hear hoots and hollers, probably from the PupSouth guys.

I recognize a woman shoving her way to the front of the group of reporters. She has her own Streamcast channel, mostly game reviews.

"The elephant in the room is the internet sensation known as Lukezilla," she says. Tori rolls her eyes at the pun. "Luke was a crucial part of the round in Minneapolis," the woman says. "He chastised Cyrus online, went viral, got suspended for cheating, sneaked his way onto another team, and then lost to your team in the quarterfinals."

"That's not a question," Tori says. "That's a list of stuff that happened."

"Do you feel justice was served?" the reporter asks, raising her voice because the crowd noise seems to have turned up a couple notches since she mentioned my username.

"Because we beat them?" Tori asks over the din. "No, we didn't look at it that way. They were just the next team to play. There was nothing personal in it. We're friends with all of them."

"But it must have been pretty sweet, after all the drama, to be the ones to eliminate him from the competition." The reporter is clearly fishing for the sound bite she wants.

"It's always sweet to win," Tori says. Max nods eagerly behind her. "But there's nothing vindictive in it."

"Do you think Lukezilla breached the user agreement?"

"How would I know?" Tori asks.

Because you know me, I want to protest.

"What about the rest of you?" The journalist eyes Zach, Noah, and Max. "Is Luke a cheater?"

Zach shakes his head. "His name is Lucas. And no way," he says. "He got hacked. Everybody knows it, and they know why."

"Because of his viral video," the journalist suggests.

"Yes," says Zach. "And the drama isn't his fault. The drama is everyone else fanning the flames." He lays a lot of emphasis on the last part, clearly meaning the reporter is part of the problem.

"If you think he's innocent," she asks, "why did you proceed in the tournament without him?"

"Because we wanted to play," Max says, sounding defensive.

"It's not our fault if Lucas got himself in the crossfire of the internet. What were we *supposed* to do?" He gives me a hard look.

The reporter starts to answer, but Max holds up a hand. "Any questions about the people who are *on* our team?"

There aren't. Max turns and walks away. Tori and Max follow. Zach is left alone, looking the way he does when he cruises the hallways. Like he's expecting a fight and will start one if he has to. He notices me and waves.

"Lucas, my dude, get up here," he says. Heads swivel, and all eyes are on me. I don't want to do this, but I walk over next to him and he throws an arm around me.

"Lucas has put up with way too much," he says. "All he did was stick up for a friend, and a bunch of people lost their minds. And he showed up to play today, even with all the hate. He made it deep in the competition with everybody booing him. And look at him? He's still chill. Because he's a tank. He can take a lot of damage."

There's an honest-to-God round of applause. Everybody's got their phones snapping, taking our picture. I probably look like I got smacked in the face with a dead fish. Because while my best buddies all wandered off, here's the school bully standing beside me, the guy I didn't want on the team, and the most annoying car-trip companion in history. *He's* the one sticking up for me.

• • •

"Want to get pizza again when we go back?" I ask Zach as we bus to the hotel. Even national champions take the bus sometimes. It's after seven, and I figure Isaac and Yolanda have already eaten because old people eat dinner early.

"I was going to see if the girls want to go," he says.

"Oh yeah." I forgot about the ballerinas. "Don't they have a mom with them?"

"We're all big kids. We can go across the street for pizza," he says. "Anyway, it doesn't hurt to ask."

"True." I try to act like dining out in a strange city with girls I barely know is normal for me. "By the way," I say, because I feel like I owe him something, "I really appreciate what you did back there."

"You mean win?"

"I mean what you said to the reporter," I tell him.

"Oh yeah. Well, you know. It really kind of stinks how everyone treated you. And you helped me get to Chicago and everything. Even though I was always a jerk to you at school. I don't know why I was." He thinks it over. "Honestly, it was because I knew we were into the same stuff and could be buds but you were already tight with M and N and didn't need anyone else. So I was jealous." He says it all slowly. He's live-streaming his own thoughts. "Anyway, I figured I should stick up for you today."

"Well, thanks," I say.

"You're welcome," he says. And then, in a burst of breath, he says, "Tori hacked you."

"What?"

"She made this app, to check your status on the leaderboard from your phone."

"Yeah . . . ? I haven't used that app in ages."

"Well, she used it to capture your password, which I guess you never change, because she was able to use it a couple days ago to log into *Smashtown* and run some XP boosts. And she was super obvious about it, so it would catch the attention of Kogeki Games and get you suspended."

"Tori would never do that," I say. My mind is somersaulting. Would she do it, though? So she could play in the tournament?

Would she do it if she was insanely jealous because her team didn't make it?

Would she do it if she was crushing hard on Jacob and wanted to keep hanging around with him in Chicago instead of taking in the sights with her parents?

"I'm as shocked as you are," Zach says.

"Are you sure?" I ask Zach.

"Yes. During one of the breaks today, Max said something, and Noah—"

"Said what?" I interrupt.

"He said, 'Those hackers are super smart,' because Noah was talking about brute-forcing passwords. He says he's seen you log in and knows you have a long password, like twenty characters *at least*."

"Yeah. Twenty-four actually."

"He said he doesn't know how anybody hacked you because it takes infinity to brute force a password like that. Then Max says, 'Yeah, those hackers are super smart,' and he kind of looked at Tori, and Noah noticed. He says 'OMG—You guys did it?' And they didn't deny it! First they tried to pretend it was a joke. But Noah and I didn't buy it. So Tori says, 'What are you going to do? Tell the judges? Get us all thrown out?' And Max says, 'Look, he deserved it for going on his soapbox and bringing all the hate down on us. He didn't ask any of *us* for permission, did he? He was making a decision for the entire team.' And Tori says, 'Hey, it's really my team anyway, if you remember who actually founded it.'"

I am absolutely at a loss for words. I've known Max since first grade. Him and Noah both. We were all in the same class. During the first week, the teacher, who we called Mr. G., asked the class what we wanted to be when we grew up. All three of us said 'gamers,' and we knew we were meant to be buddies for life. Since then we've always hung out together and been there for each other.

But now Max has betrayed me, and Noah knew and didn't say anything, which means *he* betrayed me too.

"Sorry," Zach tells me. "They're going to be so mad I told you." He gives me a pleading look. "Don't tell them I told you?"

I shake my head. "I won't," I say. There's nothing to gain from it. It's not like they're going to replay the entire tournament. "But thanks for telling me. You're a true friend." I fight back tears. There's no way I'm crying on a bus in front of a bunch of strangers. Well, I did that earlier, but there's no way I'm crying in front of Zach.

He rolls his eyes and changes the subject.

"So, who do you think is cuter? Olivia or Sophie?"

• • •

Isaac is still in his shirt and tie, but the tie is loosened and the top buttons of his shirt are undone, so you can see the white cotton tee underneath. He's relaxing in the armchair. Zach has gone to invite the girls to dinner. Apparently, he knows their room number.

"Did you already eat?" I ask Isaac. "We're going to get pizza." To be honest, I'm not sure I can—I feel like rolling up in a ball and never talking to anyone ever again after what Zach told me, but Zach thinks the pizza and girls will take my mind off things.

"Uh," he says, thinking it over. "No, we didn't have dinner. Yolanda's napping in her room. She has a migraine."

"Oh, I'm sorry. Are you hungry?"

"A bit," he says. "But I'm pretty tired."

"Yeah, me too. How did it go with your mom?"

"It got better," he says. "We talked. . . ." He doesn't seem to have the energy to tell me more. "What did you do with your day? See the sights?" he asks instead.

"I went back to the tournament. I managed to get back into it, but my team didn't win." I leave it at that. I know how Isaac feels—I'm too tired to explain too. "At least I got to play."

"That's good," he said. "I'm glad you're here. I was feeling lonesome."

A moment later the door beeps from the key card, and Zach comes in.

"They're going to meet us there," he says excitedly. "Sophie's mom is going to be there. They thought it was supercool that I won."

"Uh . . ." Suddenly I don't think I should go. "I'm gonna hang with Isaac. Yolanda's not feeling well, and he's kind of alone."

"Really? What about dinner?"

"Could you bring us back something?"

"Are you sure? I think they'll be kind of bummed if you don't go," Zach says. "You're the famous one."

"What? *You're* the champion."

"One of them," he says. "One of the champions. Come on!" I realize for all his bluster, he *is* in over his head with the big-city date night and needs backup. But Isaac needs me more, I decide.

"Sorry," I tell Zach.

"That's OK," he says. "What do you want me to bring you back?" he asks. "And can I borrow one of your nice shirts? I didn't bring any."

"Sure. There's one more in my suitcase. Lucky for you, you're almost as short as me."

He puts on the cream-colored one, straightens the collar, then rakes his curly hair with one hand.

"Lookin' good," I tell him. "Oh, and ask the restaurant if they can make a couple cream cheese and green olive sandwiches." There's sandwiches on the menu, so I figure they can. "On rye bread if they have it."

"What?"

I repeat the instructions. "Two of them," I tell him. "One

for me and one for Isaac. But also some fries for me. And a chocolate shake." I give him forty bucks from my wallet. I actually haven't come close to using all my prize money from Minneapolis, even after giving Yolanda gas money.

"Sure. Text me if you need anything else, bud," he says. He whaps my shoulder and is gone. I fall onto the sofa. I look at Isaac, who looks back at me. We sit like that in silence for a while.

"I have a Ross Cooper book. Want me to read some?"

He nods.

I pull the book out of my backpack. "We could use a couple cats."

"That's all I ever wanted," he says.

PART 3
SMASHTOWN

CHAPTER 15

Yolanda has brought an audiobook for the trip back. It's about a retired police detective named Gabe who gets wrapped up in a mystery when one of his old friends from the force is arrested. I fade in and out of sleep and can't follow the story. Zach watches every video recap and commentary of his victory, his headphones plugged in and volume blessedly low, while he trades texts with someone. Maybe the ballerinas, his mom, or the other 4LMNTs.

It only occurs to me when Yolanda drops me off in front of my house that she didn't threaten to throw us out of the car even once the whole way back. We got along fine.

Mom sweeps me into a bear hug the moment I get in the door.

"Honey, why didn't you tell us?" she asks, then squeezes me again before I can answer. Dad steps in and hugs both of us. He basically hugs our hug.

She can't know about Tori and Max, so she must mean the meme. *That's not funny!*

"I thought you might keep me from the tournament," I say, but my voice is muffled by the hug.

"You shouldn't have gone through it alone," Mom says after we separate. "You need to *tell us* if you're harassed and bullied online."

"I wasn't bullied," I tell her. "It was just a meme. It wasn't personal."

"But it has to hurt," she says. "Do you want to talk about it?"

"Not right now."

"It doesn't have to be with us," she says. "It could be a professional."

"What, like a pro gamer?"

"No," she says, confused. "I mean a pro at helping kids with their problems."

"Like a psychiatrist?" I can't believe she thinks it's that serious.

"A therapist," she says.

"Isn't that for kids with real problems?"

"Being bullied is a real problem!"

"I don't know. I don't think so. I'm fine."

I haul my suitcase up to my room, unzip it, and throw all the clothes into the hamper, including my favorite polo shirt that Zach dripped tomato sauce on and probably ruined. I realize I'm shaking and sit down on the bed. Something about Mom's words got to me.

It *did* hurt to be treated like a joke. I'd been pretending it didn't, but it did. I was able to shove it outside my mind as long as I had the trip and the tournament to think about. Now that's all over, but that meme is still with me. It'll be with me forever. In twenty years I'll be a middle-age guy with a job and maybe a family, and people will still be posting that meme. "That's not funny!" will haunt me forever.

I could have told Mom I'm a tank and can take a lot of damage. But I feel pretty squishy all of a sudden.

• • •

The next day I open the official ticket to complain about my account being suspended. It takes me at least an hour to write up the explanation. My phone chimes while I write it. It's Gabby.

Got home OK. You?

Yep, I reply. We text for a while, mostly about the tournament. I almost tell her about Mom thinking I need therapy, but don't. I'm not quite ready to tell anyone outside the family. Then Gabby has to go do something, and I go back to my form.

The phone chimes again. This time it's Zach.

Wanna hang out this week?

Sure. Just text me tomorrow

Will do, bro

I read back over the form. I think I hit all the major points. I hit send. My phone chimes *a third* time. It's Mom.

You good over there?

Yep.

The fourth chime is Dad, asking the same question. They're both at work and worried about me being home alone.

What I want is for texts or calls from Max or Noah. They don't know I know, so there's no reason they wouldn't text me. They used to do it at least once a day. But they don't, so I don't either. I don't know what I'd say to them anyway.

• • •

I drop in on Isaac the next day. I find him sitting in the dark room. No audiobook playing. As usual, Yolanda uses the time to slip out and go manage her own life.

"How's it going?" I ask.

"S'all right," he says. "My mother called yesterday."

"No kidding?"

"First time in a long time. I guess we're talking again."

"That's great."

"She said she would give my book another try, but we couldn't find a copy. I think I got rid of every copy."

"Uh . . ." He's forgotten I have it, and I lent it to Cyrus's boss. "I'm sure it'll turn up," I tell him. He nods.

I sit down. Petey finds me and leaps into my lap. I realize I've missed him.

"You know, even listening to books is harder than it used to be," Isaac says. "I can't remember what happened in the last chapter. I don't know what to do with myself anymore."

"I'm sorry, Isaac. Maybe it'll get better?"

"I don't think many people get better at my age," he says.

I've wanted to ask a couple questions for a long time. Like, if Isaac was ever married, or even had a girlfriend. It's hard to imagine him young, let alone in love. Of course I know he could have had a *boyfriend*, back when it would have been top secret and maybe even illegal, but that's also hard to imagine. He's so solitary. It seems like he just wants his books and cats and that's all.

Instead I tell him what Tori and Max did to me. For some reason it's easier than talking to mom or dad or my friends . . . because he's once removed from everything else in my life, because he doesn't interrupt, because he doesn't try to make me see things from another point of view, and because he doesn't want to give me advice. He doesn't even ask questions, even though I'm *sure* he doesn't get the technical part. I realize that having friends cheat and lie is a million times worse than cyberbullying, or whatever you want to call the meme and the jokes and the boos.

"*People,*" is all he says when I'm finally done dumping it all on him.

"Yeah. People." No wonder he prefers cats.

• • •

On Wednesday, Zach's mom drops us off at a park with a beach and a net-climbing course. We kick around in the surf, race to the top of the nets, then eat Popsicles in the rec center. Zach tells me the texts from the ballerinas have petered out, but it's fine, because he can't date a girl in another city. I don't tell him I've been trading texts with Gabby in Wilmington, Delaware, and that I think she's pretty cool.

Some people are all right, I decide. Zach and Gabby, for example.

"So, have you smashed any noobs since getting back?" I ask him. I haven't, because my old account is still suspended. Besides, who would I play with? The KidsfromSLP have Jacob back, and the 4LMNTs are dead to me. I wouldn't go back if they asked, but they haven't asked.

"Nah, we're all taking a break," he tells me. "But I'm kind of off the team anyway."

"Really? They kicked you off?"

"More like I quit," he says. He pauses, pretending to need to get every last drip from his SpongeBob-shaped ice-cream treat. "OK, so it was mutual," he says at last. There must be more to the story he's not telling. He flips his Popsicle stick at the trash can across the room. It banks off the wall and lands in the can. He holds both arms up, signaling a touchdown. "Two points!"

"Wrong sport," I tell him. He shrugs that he doesn't care.

"So are you going to watch Cyrus's live stream Friday?" he asks.

"I don't know. I mean, yeah. It is a new *Smashtown* game. I want to see it. There's new characters and stuff. But dude, you can *play*." I think enviously of the early access the winners of the tourney were given.

"Yeah, I guess. But I'll watch first."

My phone beeps with a message from Gabby.

OMG he did it again.

Who did what? I ask.

Cyrus.

I open the Streamcast app on my phone and play the latest from Cyrus, who is in the middle of a live stream.

"... so we're counting down to my live video of *Smashtown Fury* ...," he's saying. Zach nudges me, so I set the phone on the table. "That will start in about ..." Cyrus taps his wrist, which doesn't have a watch. "... Fifty-five hours. The guys at Kogeki tell me I'll be up for at least a day, maybe longer. So I'd better rest up until then. But I do want to answer questions about the game. Ask away." You can see his eyes look downward as he follows the flood of questions scrolling by.

"A lot of you want to know if *Fury* is an action adventure game like *Frontiers*, or a battle arena like *Frenzy*. I haven't seen it yet, but the guys at Kogeki tell me you can run missions by yourself, but you might run into other players. Whether those players are friends or foes is up to you. You can team up and split the loot or simply blast them off the map and take the loot for yourself. If you think this will lead to lots of backstabbing and treachery, you might be right." He winks.

Then it's a good game for Max and Tori, I think bitterly.

But what did Cyrus do again? There's only one thing Gabby would text me about. I pause the stream and rewind.

"Hey, I was watching that," Zach says.

"Give me a minute." I can see the thumbnail as I rewind. Cyrus's face is midboil. He's "stroking out." I let it play, picking up at the end.

"They made me stop that during the tour," he says. "You know, corporate partners. Impressionable children. But this isn't the tour. It's my show, and I can do whatever I want. Woot!"

It's good to be back." And he repeats the face-boil to show how good it is. "What can I say?" Cyrus says with a dramatic shrug. "I don't like being told what to do."

"He did that dumb stroke thing," Zach whispers.

"You used to think it was funny."

"Meh, I'm over it," he says.

I tap the LIVE button to rejoin the live broadcast.

"Next question is, will I be playing by myself," Cyrus is saying. "It is multiplayer, but I, of course, will be playing it by myself, *I think*. But who knows? Maybe somebody will show up? That's part of the fun. Five hundred something other people have access, and all they have to do is land on the same server."

I quickly type up a reply and hit send.

Cyrus, it's Lukezilla. That's still not funny!

I feel like it's casting a bottle into the ocean, hoping it makes its way to the right island, but Cyrus holds up a finger in a "wait a second" gesture.

"Oh wow, I have a comment from the internet-famous funniness expert, Lukezilla." He laughs. "Listen, buddy. I do what I do. You don't have to watch, all right?"

That's not the point, I write.

"Lukezilla, seriously. I like you. You're a good kid, a bit intense, but that's OK. A *much* better gamer than a lot of people appreciate. But if you're going to barge in on every Streamcast to scold me . . . that's no way to live, Lukezilla." Now he's leaning in, gesturing, imploring me.

How about I barge in to your game play video and beat you to the finish line? I type. I see his eyes flicker with surprise as he reads it.

"Oh wow!" He covers his mouth. "Lukezilla wants to tango." He rubs his chin thoughtfully. "And you have about a one in a gazillion chance of landing on the same server and finding me. But sure, Lukezilla. I can't wait to see you. And with that, I think I'll hang up and get some shut-eye, Cyborgs, because apparently this will be more interesting than I thought. Bye-bye!" The stream stops.

"Dude, what did you do?" Zach says.

"You saw. Will you let me use your account?"

"Heck, yeah. I can't wait to see this. Dude, how are you going to find him?"

"I don't know. I'll figure it out."

And now my phone is beeping like mad. I have messages from Lia, from Jacob, from Nash. And one from Gabby.

U R MY HERO!!!

What have I got myself into?

• • •

I show up on Noah's doorstep early on Thursday. I know he never goes anywhere before noon unless he has to. I also know—and for this I am now grateful—that he doesn't watch Cyrus Popp.

"Oh. Hey, Lucas." Noah does not sound thrilled to see me. He might suspect I know about the hacking, but we're also officially still friends, and dropping in on each other isn't that unusual. "How's it going?" he asks as we walk to his room, which is on the first floor. His room is the tidiest you've ever seen for a teenage boy. Books alphabetical on the shelves, finished Lego sets without a brick out of place. A chess set out on the desk, in the middle of a match.

"Playing yourself?" I ask, gesturing.

"A kid in India," he says. "We send our moves by mail. Old school, letters and stamps. It's taking forever. We could play on an app, but this is more fun somehow."

I jokingly swap a couple pieces and swap them back.

"Nice try," he says. "I have the whole board in my head." He taps it.

"You have a good memory."

"Photographic," he says.

"You must never forget a password?" I ask.

"Nope," he says.

"What if it was a twenty-character string of letters and numbers that you happened to see for a few seconds?"

Noah looks uncomfortable.

"Look, Lucas, I don't know your password, and I sure wouldn't use it if I did."

"I'm not saying you did," I tell him. "Didn't even occur to me. My friends would never do that." I try to keep the sarcasm out of my voice.

"Oh." He lets out a deep breath. "Sorry, I felt like you were accusing me of something."

"I am," I admit. "But not of hacking me. But I'll bet you memorized Jacob's dad's access code to the *Smashtown* servers."

"So *that's* what you want. Yes, I was able to remember it long enough to write it down when I got home."

"No kidding? Can I have a peek?"

"I haven't even used it," he says, going to his desk. He flips through index cards in a plastic case, finds one, and hands it to me. I glance at it. It seems right. I wonder what's on all those other cards he has in the box. Other secret codes and passwords he's learned? Does he find them and pin them like beetles in a shadow box?

I hold the card in one hand and my phone in the other, zeroing in for a picture. He waves at me not to bother.

"Keep it," he says. "I'm not going to use it for anything. But don't get Jacob in trouble."

"You didn't worry about getting in trouble when we all played on those dedicated servers."

"Er, no. But we were practicing. I don't know what you're up to now."

"Smashing noobs," I say innocently.

I try the code as soon as I get home. It still works. I call up the list of servers. I don't know which one Cyrus will be using. Also, I can't log in, because my account is still suspended, but I could use Zach's, probably.

CHAPTER 16

REQUEST DENIED.

The answer has come from Kogeki Games, followed by reasons I might have had my account suspended, all of which are things I didn't do.

I didn't hope for anything better. It's all right. I have a backup plan, which is to play under Zach's account. He's OK'd it and sent me his password. After all those practice sessions and tournaments, he's cracked level forty, meaning I can play as Trunkzilla.

But I've put off the hardest part of this plan, which is telling Mom and Dad I plan to stay up all night playing a video game.

To their credit, they hear me out. They really listen. But a fat lot of good it does me.

"You are *not* staying up for who-knows-how-many hours the weekend before school starts," Mom says. "Not that you could even if school wasn't starting," she quickly adds.

"We know you like these games, buddy, but we gave you

a long leash this summer. I mean, you went to *Chicago* by yourself."

"I wasn't by myself! I was with two grown-ups!"

"That's not the point. You've got to have priorities, kiddo. Now, school becomes the number one priority."

My number one priority is saving face, but "I told the internet I would!" is not a good argument in the eyes of parents. I need to translate it into terms they understand.

"If I don't, I'll be memed again." I probably would too. "I'll be cyberbullied some more."

"Oh, honey," Mom says, "if that happens, you don't have to go online at all."

"When a kid is bullied a school, you don't stop sending him to school."

"We'd find a different school," Dad says. "We certainly wouldn't encourage you to go to the school and stay up all night to make some kind of point."

"Well there's only one internet!" I say. I realize I'm sinking fast. "Look, what about this? Dad says school is a priority. I'll beat the game this weekend, and then I'll quit. Until . . ." A week doesn't seem long enough. ". . . until winter break," I tell them, shocked at my own suggestion. But if the stakes are that high—three whole months without gaming—then maybe they'll see how important this is to me.

Mom shakes her head. Either she's rejecting the deal or she doesn't believe me.

"I need to do this," I tell them.

Mom sighs. Dad drums his fingers impatiently. They hate

begging. *I* hate begging. But if they say no, I'll lock myself in my room and barricade the door. If they take my laptop, I'll leave home, borrow a laptop, and play under a bridge, if I can find one with an outlet and Wi-Fi.

"Please? I'll never ask for anything ever again?"

"I'm through talking about it," Mom says, getting up. "Let your father decide."

Dad doesn't get up. I guess that means I can keep pleading my case.

"Dad, remember when we dropped in on Isaac and I called an ambulance and saved his brain and maybe his life?"

"Yeah, I remember that," he says dryly. "Trying to cash in your karma, huh?"

"Not exactly. But that's what started all this. We saw Isaac, I told the internet about it, and I got memed. One thing led to another. And it's led me here."

Dad seems to be thinking it over. I feel like I've almost won, but I need that critical hit. "I can't give up now. If I do, I'm a joke, and if I'm a joke, my video was a joke. And if the video is a joke, Isaac is a joke."

Dad sighs. "Fine, but you have to be done by Saturday at nine p.m.," he says. "And you won't play at all on Sunday."

That's a bit more than twenty-four hours, and more than I expected, although it's probably not enough to beat the game. But I'll fight that boss when I get to it.

"It's a deal," I quickly agree.

• • •

Most of the gaming forums think I won't be able to even get into the game, let alone find Cyrus. Meanwhile, Kogeki has leaked names and images of the new characters. There's Saber, a prehistoric-looking tigress assassin. A tusked, whiskered boar tank named Crankee. Lampyra, a firefly support character—nothing but speculation about what her buff will be, but people figure it has to do with light. And a cannon named Wyrm who looks like a legless, wingless dragon who squirts slime from either end. People mostly like the first three, but argue about whether Wyrm is the best or the worst character ever.

It projectile poops slime, a guy says in one forum. *Disgusting.*

I know. Isn't it awesome? is the first response.

A couple weeks ago I would have been thrilled that they were adding new levels and new characters to unlock. But I now have to create a new account and grind out the first forty levels before I get access to the new ones, so it'll be months before *I* can squirt slime out of my butt. It's not like I'll keep on using Zach's account forever.

In addition to those four there's a fifth new character. In the reveal, it is a shadow with a big question mark. Based on the ordering up until now, it could be an assassin character, but who knows? It's all alone in a tier and might be some kind of über-fighter.

The trailer says we'll meet them all during Cyrus Popp's live Streamcast event, which means I might be facing off against Saber and Crankee, getting slimed by Wyrm, and discovering the identity of the secret level forty-five character before the new mission is done.

• • •

The morning of the big day, I drop in and see Isaac. I take care of the cat boxes and return his book. I got it back in an overnight delivery, with a sticky note that simply said *LOVED IT*—C.

"I thought I burned every copy of that," he says. Which is exactly what he said the last time I pulled it out of my backpack.

"You were going to send it to your mother," I remind him. Then I remember it was Yolanda I talked to about that. But he knows what I mean.

"That's right. She's going to read it again. Or have somebody at the home read it to her." He nods. "Did you make up with your friends?"

"Nope." I'm blown away that he remembers *that*.

"Oh well. Do you want to read me more of that book?" He means the one I started at the hotel. I don't have it with me.

"I can't. I have to go home and nap. I, uh, have a big night in front of me." I do not think Isaac will understand live-streaming a speed run of a new video game. And that gives me an out-of-nowhere thought.

"Can I borrow something?" I ask him.

• • •

I have never been a speed gamer. I prefer to go slow and explore, enjoy the environment, search for loot, and find Easter eggs. But I've prepped the best I can, watching videos with tips for speed runners. I nap and wake up an hour before showtime.

I have plenty of snacks and beverages on hand. I line up my *Smashtown* vinyl figurines for support, in level order, keeping Trunky within reach in case I need to tap him for luck.

I'll be TMI on one thing: I'll allow myself bathroom breaks, like Cyrus does. Sometimes there are three minutes of live video showing an empty swivel chair still rocking from his quick departure.

I've thought a lot about what I'll wear. I mean, people will only see my head and neck, but I decide on the cream-colored polo shirt, because the orange stain from Zach's pizza date isn't visible. I've decided not to wear my fishing cap. I need to be myself, not Cyrus. Instead, I wear Isaac's plaid drivers cap. That's what I borrowed from him this morning. Not that I want to be *Isaac*, but since I'm doing this for him, I want to have a symbol. It fits better than the fishing cap and looks pretty good, I think.

At six minutes to game time, I sign in to Streamcast and begin a new stream, but pause the screen-sharing for now. After a lot of testing, I've angled the webcam and lights perfectly.

At five minutes to game time, I launch the game, enter the access code, and scan the list of servers for *Smashtown Fury*. There are dozens of live servers for the new content, easy to ID because they all begin with "fury," but I don't know which one Cyrus is using. I could trial-and-error it for hours.

A private message pops up in my Streamcast chat.

Find me in xxx8761, it says. It's from Cyrus. I don't know how he knows I can see the dedicated servers. Maybe it's a lucky guess?

Thx, I reply. *Why would you tell me?*

More fun, he writes back.

I find and click the server ending in those digits and dive in to *Smashtown Fury.*

Out of habit, I sign in as Lukezilla and type in my password. I don't even *know* my password, but my fingers do, if that makes sense. And—for some reason—it works. My account is back! I'm Lukezilla!

There's no time to wonder why.

I choose Trunkzilla as my character, and click past the warning that I must finish or fail the mission before I can change characters or choose another mission. I unpause the screen sharing, take a deep breath, and begin.

"Hi, it's me," I tell the seven hundred people who are already watching. The messages start flowing.

Can't wait to LOL at the noob

Hey, it's FAILzilla

That's not funny!

I dock the chat window so I won't be distracted.

The clock ticks down to the official start time.

3 . . . 2 . . .

Dad pops in the door.

1 . . .

"Good luck, buddy!"

BATTLE!

• • •

I drop into the familiar hub of *Smashtown* Central, an octagonal block where streets converge. Next to me is a fox like no fox I've ever seen, even in video games. He's huge, with rippling muscles and long, white teeth. He turns and sneers at me. He's wearing a long-billed fishing cap! He must be the mysterious level forty-five character. A fox created in tribute to Cyrus, which he's now using for the live stream.

I chase after him, but the fox is much faster than my elephant.

Yellow signs direct me to the southeast. An area previously clogged up with rubble and wrecked cars has been cleared and signs point me farther down.

Furious Fields

Text appears at the top left:

Main Quest Updated: Find Furious Fields.

I remember that my audience hasn't heard anything from me but keyboard clicks for a while. I make up some commentary, knowing that I have to narrate my thinking to keep my audience with me.

"Well, here I am. I guess the new stuff is this way," I tell the audience. "In hot pursuit of a fox I *think* is being played by Cyrus. And this fox is the mysterious forty-fifth character." I could check his livestream if I had another screen handy. It occurs to me that *he* might have a second computer showing *my* stream. That's what a pro would do. A pro with enough money to have several computers lying around.

I could also open the chat window and simply ask, but I don't. I know it's him.

I reach some barricades with yellow and black warning stripes. I stomp through and follow the path past rubble, the usual mix of building materials, metal scraps, and other refuse that shapes the corridors and mazes in the game. This time I see there are bones among the refuse.

"Looks like the Furious Fields are so popular, people are dying to get in," I say, using a joke Dad makes whenever we drive past a cemetery. I turn a corner and reach a tall barbed wire fence with a locked gate. A sign warns that the gate is electric.

"OK, first real challenge," I say. "I learned the hard way in Chicago that you don't want to tangle with the fences. So I guess I better find a way to get that gate open. There's a gate house with a lever but no way to get over there."

There is a clamor of barks and baying sounds over my headphones, and a trio of dogs appears, guarding the gate, snarling and drooling and looking enraged. They look like Pinchers, those doberman characters, but they're way bigger. Mutant, overgrown Pinchers.

"New NPCs," I tell the audience. "Nonplayer characters," I add, on the outside chance some of them are total noobs. "And a hint to the backstory. More DNA-splicing experiments in the *Smashtown* science labs. Hmmm." I prowl back and forth along the fence. The environment resets after about three minutes, so Cyrus must have flown past this part several minutes ago.

"The bones," I suddenly recall out loud. I turn back and find a few can be picked up and stored in my inventory. I run back to the fence.

"So, I'm supposed to trick the dogs into opening the gate for me? Yeah, that's it." I return to where the guardhouse is. "Yep, there's a hole in the fence here, perfectly lined up with the broken window in the gatehouse. . . ." I take a bone from the inventory, hit the key to aim, line up the hole in the fence with the one in the gatehouse, and toss it in with my trunk. The bone bounces off the gatehouse and is snatched up by one of the dogs. I hit the sweet spot with the second bone and get it through the window. One of the dogs leaps at the window, barking. It still can't get in.

I know the answer to the puzzle is to get a dog to hurl its body through the window and hit the switch, but knowing how to solve a problem and actually doing it are different things. I've learned that over and over playing games. Also—a bit—in real life.

"I'm supposed to smash out the rest of the window," I say out loud. I do so, finding a rock among the rubble that can be picked up and thrown. "I have to get it past Jumpy McBarker over there." I zoom the rock past its head and shatter the glass. The dog scrambles in after the bone I lobbed in earlier and hits the lever, as I expected. The gate opens enough for a smaller character to get through, but it's a tight fit for a tank.

"Thanks, Kogeki," I mutter, and squeeze through the tight gap. I get through and remember there's a third dog when it attacks me.

"Here, boy," I say, tossing the last bone. "I guess I could have walloped him," I explain to the audience, "but I don't like hurting animals if I don't have to."

And on the mission goes. I still don't know what the objective is, but there's nothing to do but keep moving and exploring—and hoping Cyrus isn't leaps and bounds in front of me. Three hours go by. There are battles against mutant uglies, a few puzzles, and lots of pathfinding. I make my way to the outskirts of town and into a desolate suburb. At last, text appears at the top saying that the quest to find Furious Fields is accomplished.

"Yay," I say dryly. "Lovely place for a picnic." The so-called fields are a wasteland of weedy undergrowth and litter. A bit farther along the path splits into three, each with a sign and arrow pointing down a different path.

CEASELESS SAVANNA

RANCOR PRAIRIE

STEPPE OF RECKONING

"They all sound so pleasant," I tell my audience—up to five digits now, I see by glancing at the Streamcast strip at the bottom of my screen. "I don't know what to do first. I guess I'll take them in order."

I take the branch to the left, the Ceaseless Savanna.

"I hope I at least learn what the goal is to this mission," I say. "Wait, what's that?" I see a shadow moving weakly off to the side. I come closer and find a wrinkled, misshapen beetle-like creature, bigger than I am. Big, but wiry and green. This one seems to be in a lot of pain and barely alive. It brings itself up and mumbles something at me.

"I could take him out," I think out loud, "but I don't think he'll hurt me. Let's find what he has to say."

I use key commands to crouch and listen.

A cutscene starts.

"Please," it gasps, "bring me to Nightfall Swamp. I want to die at home."

Text bleeps across the top.

MAIN QUEST UPDATED: FIND PATH THROUGH SAVANNA.

SIDE QUEST UNLOCKED: BRING LAMPYRA TO NIGHTFALL SWAMP.

"Great," I tell my audience. "An escort mission. I *hate* escort missions." But it's a side quest, which means it's optional. And it might be a trick?

"No time for this. Onward," I announce. The beetle cries out to me as I walk away.

"Please . . . please . . ."

"I know it's pretty pathetic, but it's not a real being," I remind myself, and my audience, now more than 12,000 people.

"Help—*gasp*—me, and I'll tell you a secret," the bug pleads.

"Fine." I turn Trunky back. "I have to get across this field anyway. But how am I supposed to carry this guy?"

The firefly leaps up and wraps its frail arms around Trunky's neck. Trunky staggers under the weight of the giant bug, then stands, stooped over, the creature slung across his back. We enter a maze of corridors shaped by the rubble and weeds.

"I thought savannas were wide open spaces," I grumble as I steer Trunkzilla s-l-o-w-l-y through the maze, guess which way to go, find a dead end, turn back, and try a different path. I realize the weight of the beetle thing depletes Trunky's health, so every few minutes I set it down, wait for Trunky's health to climb back up, then let the beetle leap onto his back again. There are various obstacles to get past, and the whole expedition grinds on for more than an hour. It's almost midnight when Mom and Dad pop in.

"Still doing all right?" they ask.

"Sure." I mean, it's going horrible *gamewise*, because I've gotten lured into a long side quest, but otherwise . . .

"You must be tired," Mom says.

"Nah," I say. "My irritation is working like caffeine."

They both laugh. Mom comes over and gives me a quick hug, on camera.

"Mom!"

"What's that?" she says. "Twenty-four thousand viewers!"

"Yeah, I guess."

"All those kids staying up past their bedtime."

"Mom!"

Some mutant winged monkeys fly over the fence.

"Gotta go!" I tell her, pulling free of the hug in real life at the same time Trunky shrugs the firefly off so he can go on offense.

Trunky fights off the monkey birds, picking up rocks and rubble and flinging them at the creatures as they zoom in to pinch and punch him. I dance Trunky around to avoid stepping on the firefly, which they are clearly trying to either kill or carry off. It's a long battle, but I finally prevail, taking out enough monkeys that the rest go screeching away.

"I'm having flashbacks to *The Wizard of Oz*," I tell the audience. "I saw it when I was five and *still* have nightmares."

I let Trunky's health creep up, let the bug leap on his back, and trudge on. I see an exit and thunder forward, realizing as I emerge that I'm back at the mouth of the maze.

"Nooooo!" I wail. Somewhere, Cyrus is probably through one and a half of these three missions, and I'm still stuck on a side quest. I'm sure if I opened my chat window I'd find lots of people updating me on Cyrus's progress, but I don't want to get sucked into reading about Cyrus when I have my own game to play.

Of course, people are also probably telling him what *I'm* up to, and he might be reading it, but I can't worry about that.

"The maze doesn't make sense," I think out loud. "There must be a pattern to solve it." I reenter and pay closer attention to the subtle details of the walls and rubble, noting when I'm routed in a circle.

"So it's up, right, down, down . . ." I say. I grab a paper and pen and jot it all down. Still, it's another half hour before I emerge from the far side of the maze. A sign points one way to Nightfall Swamp, another way to *Smashtown* Science, Inc.

I haul the firefly to the swamp, fight off another horde of flying monkeys, and finally set it on a marshy isthmus. I know it's called an isthmus because there's a sign. The text appears saying that I've finished the side quest and a cutscene starts. The beetle's abdomen flickers and glows. The firefly is lit at last. It takes a ragged breath, trying to speak.

"When the time comes to choose . . ." It coughs. Its abdomen flickers and glows. "Choose . . ." It stops to draw breath, its fragile chest rattling, and goes still.

"Choose what?" I plead.

The firefly turns to dust, leaving me in the empty cavern without anything to show for my trouble.

"What was that?" I ask aloud—maybe a little too loud, considering there are sleeping parents down the hall. "I think I got *epically* trolled by the game!"

CHAPTER 17

It's 1:20 a.m., and I feel the first wave of exhaustion. I've played way past midnight, before Mom and Dad started computer curfew, and I know it gets harder and harder as your brain and reflexes slow down. But I've never stayed up into the next day, which I'll have to do this time.

"I could have skipped the side quest and finished with the lab by now," I announce. "Well, no regrets. Because if you can't take the time to help a giant bug, it's not a game I want to win. OK, that's sour grapes, I admit. I might get a little punchy here, so please don't record this or anything."

I take a deep breath.

"So, maybe I just blew the game, but I don't want to be the kind of guy who leaves somebody to suffer," I explain. "Winning isn't everything. That's what I'm saying." I tug on the brim of my hat and think about Isaac.

"Onward through the darkness," I tell the audience.

The next mission is to find a way into the *Smashtown* Science Labs.

I find the labs and spend the next ninety minutes or so exploring, discovering story elements on blackboards, computer screens, and old tape recordings. I have to skim through them for now.

"This new content has a richer backstory than most of the *Smashtown* missions," I tell the audience—now 40,000 kids staying up past their bedtime, and maybe some in Europe waking up to begin the next day. "Wish I had time to really absorb it."

I reach a dead end and double back, then find a wall I can smash through to continue.

At the heart of the labs is a mainframe computer, which asks for a code I don't have. The code might be in the stuff I skimmed through, but there's one more room to explore first, so I burst Trunky through the door.

"Uh-oh." The room has been destroyed and there's a gaping hole left in the wall. "Obviously an experiment gone awry," I say.

Text appears on the screen.

Quest Updated: Find the Escaped Creature.

"Awesome," I announce. "Time for the first boss!" Usually games have a particularly tough opponent at the end of each level. *Smashtown* missions are no exception.

I walk Trunky through the wall and see a trail leading away from the building into a craggy wilderness beyond. There aren't any footprints. It looks more like something was dragged, gouging the ground as it went.

It is three in the morning. Every time I glance at the number of viewers, it's grown by a few hundred. 42,000, 43,000, 44,000, 45,000. . . . The excitement of a growing audience and what looks like the first boss fight gives me a surge of energy despite my exhaustion.

"Let's see what that is," I announce and plunge into the thicket.

• • •

I follow the tracks and discover some boarlike soldiers prodding a wormlike creature with electric rods. I know from the previews that the boars are called Crankees. The other creature is Wyrm, but the one in the game previews was about the size of any other cannon, and this one is ginormous, twenty times the size of Trunky.

"So we've seen Pincher grow to the size of a bear, and Spry with wings," I tell the audience. "And now a mega-Wyrm. This is what those science labs are up to, and I think my ultimate goal is to stop them. But first I have to take care of this thing."

The Wyrm wails as it gets shocked again and again.

"Or, maybe I have to *rescue* it," I think aloud.

I fight a long siege against the Crankees, which are tough-hided and hard to kill. I distract them one at a time by throwing rocks and rubble. When one comes to investigate, I take it out and then let Trunky's health go back up. It's a grind, but I finally release the monster and make the rest of them flee.

The Wyrm turns on me.

"Some gratitude!" I complain as I steer Trunky away from a spray of green slime. "But of course, I knew that this was a boss, so. Here we go."

I figure out a pattern to avoid the jets of toxic goo while Trunky deals damage, eventually sending the slimy creature off a cliff. I feel kind of sorry for it as it spirals down into the mist and disappears. But then I get over it.

"One mission down, two to go," I say, trying to sound casual but knowing how raw and tired my voice is. "I still have, uh . . ." I look at the clock. It's four-thirty a.m. I try to count the hours until nine p.m. and can't. My mind is too tired. But it feels like way more than a third of my time has passed, and I'm only through a third of the game. I think longingly of bed and sleep.

"Let's go check out the next area," I tell my 50,000 followers.

• • •

Rancor Prairie is a bit easier than the Savanna. I infiltrate a military encampment and steal an access code for a computer back at the labs. The code is in a silver box at the top of a water tower. This is the part the trailer showed, with the tigress and boar making a run at the prize.

There is a lot of stealth involved—taking keys, sneaking onto guard kiosks, and disabling security beams, all while avoiding vigilant boar guards and robotic turrets that shoot lasers. It's harder for Trunky's big body to get around than it probably is for other characters, but I have an advantage in the inevitable battles.

Mom brings me a scrambled egg and sausage muffin

sandwich and a hot cup of tea. I now have more than a hundred thousand followers—the numbers spiked fast when the sun came up in North America—and they get to watch me eat, then watch an empty chair while I run to take care of important business.

When I get back, I breach the final security zone and face the second boss; another of the boar-style guards blown up to the size of a gorilla. He flings wreckage at Trunky while I veer him around lasers and stomp off minions. After taking out the guards, I hide and watch the gorilla pitch a fit until he burns himself out and falls asleep like an overtired toddler. I sneak Trunky over and steal the key around his neck, scampering away as he wakes up and goes into a new rage. And now Trunky climbs the tower, while the gorilla follows.

"He's faster than me," I tell the audience. "But I'm an elephant, and he's an overgrown money, so go figure."

He catches up before I'm halfway up the tower. I stomp on the ladder to make him fall, then climb some more. He catches up, I stomp. Second verse same as the first, as Tori would say.

Ugh, Tori. Remembering her treachery hits me with a fresh pang, but I push it out of my mind.

At last, Trunky reaches the top. He approaches the silver box, opens it with the key, and finds a piece of paper. Scribbled on it are a series of letters and numbers. A password or something?

"I bet it unlocks that terminal back at the lab," I tell the audience. "Wish I had run this mission first!"

I walk Trunky to the ladder when a red force flies at him, hitting the elephant square in the chest. At first I think it's a fireball, then realize it's the muscle-bound fox. Cyrus. At last. He snatches the paper away and sprints for the side. I blunder after him, but Trunkzilla isn't exactly spry. The fox shimmies down the ladder and disappears far below.

"Guess I'll follow him back to the lab," I tell my followers, which have doubled since breakfast. There are now 200,000 of them. "Someone want to rewind the stream and send me the code? I'll need it in a bit!" I open the chat window so I can see it if someone sends it, while trying to ignore the steady chatter streaming by.

I take Trunky down the ladder and find a shortcut to the labs; a handcart on an old railway line. A fresh army of flying monkeys greets Trunky near the end of the line. I hurl rubble and refuse at them, picking them off one by one until they fly away. I have more than a quarter-million people watching now. It's a fraction of what Cyrus probably *started* with, still, not too shabby. But I have to battle my way back to the heart of the labs, and once I get there, I have to fight Cyrus. And after *that*, I still have a third mission to run. A wave of exhaustion and futility overwhelms me. Will all these people watch me fail?

There's a thunder of footsteps. At first, I think it's the headphones, warning of more enemies approaching. But it's real footsteps. People are storming up the stairs and into my bedroom.

"What's up?" Zach asks. "I got you a burrito." He drops a fast-food bag on my desk. Is it already lunchtime?

"And I got your code," Noah says, coming in right after Zach. "I didn't need to rewind any stream. When you need it, it's right here." He taps his head. "By the way, gorillas aren't monkeys. They're apes."

"Right. Thanks, guys."

And then, walking slowly with his head down, Max comes in. He's never looked squishier than he does right now. He knows *I know* what he did. There's no other reason he'd look like that.

"Hey," he says with a nod. His eyes are shot through with red, and I wonder if he's been up all night watching. "Sorry about . . . what happened," he says vaguely. "Tori and I told Kogeki. We're both banned forever, but you got your account back."

So that explains why I got in.

"We can talk later," he says. "You're kind of busy at the moment."

"Yeah. Good to see you." But Max is right. We'll definitely talk later. He's not off the hook. But first, I have a game to win. "Good to see you guys too," I tell Zach and Noah.

I feel reenergized. I smash and bash Trunky to the center of the lab.

Max sits on the bed, Noah kneels on the floor right next to me, and Zach stands behind me like a boxing coach, kneading my shoulders.

"You got this, dude," he says.

• • •

While I'm playing, Zach catches me up on what Cyrus has been doing. His fox character is named Vyrus, he tells me.

I guess he tells everyone, because the mic is on.

"He's got the attack of an assassin and the toughness of a tank," Zach says, awed. "He's the strongest character they ever made."

"But you can't use him in battle mode," Max says. "Only on missions."

"He's like the ultimate trophy of the game," Noah throws in.

After sprinting ahead of me at the very beginning of the game, Vyrus hid behind some of the rubble, watched me get past the guard dogs, then followed while they were still gnawing on their bones. He shadowed me as I took out the enemies in front of us and cleared the path for him, staying far enough back that I never knew he was there but close enough that the game didn't reset.

"He's been gliding through and laughing at you the whole time," Max tells me.

"But he also admits you're smashing like nobody's business," Zach adds.

"So he's been playing me for a chump," I say. Of course all this is on mic.

"Yeah, but, dude. Everybody's rooting for you," Max says. "*Practically* everybody. You're totally owning this game."

"A lot of his fans started following you," Zach tells me. "And you can see his numbers drop as yours go up. They're not just watching you. They're watching you *instead* of Cyrus."

"Thanks, everybody!" I shout into the mic. "Hope I don't let you down."

I burst through the final door. Vyrus is there, accessing the mainframe. I charge. He leaps back and lets our bodies collide. We both shudder on impact. The fox snaps and slashes at me. I struggle away. Instead of pursuing me, he turns back to the mainframe.

"So while you were doing the side quest, Cyrus explored the lab and solved the secret of the game," Zach tells me (and my followers). "You can use the mainframe to evolve your character further. Go, like, mega."

"Tell me later!" I charge again, slamming the fox aside, shoving him through to the next room, the one with the ragged hole. There's a drop from the hole to the scrubby ground below. Not enough to do any real damage, but enough of a drop that a nonflying character would have to circle around through the entrance to return to this room. All I want is a little time.

The fox swipes at me and deals a lot of damage. My health meter is flashing red now, but there's nothing to do but fight on. I lay down a stomp to freeze him, then body slam the fox once more and send him sprawling out of the hole.

"Time to get amped up," Zach says excitedly. "Go! GO!"

I hurry to the room, slamming the door behind me and shoving a few things in the way as my health creeps back up. I hit the key to interact with the mainframe and am prompted for a password.

"Code?" I ask Noah.

He recites the characters and I enter them. The mainframe screen flashes to a new menu. One of them is for DNA Enhancement. Across the room I see a chamber.

"I have to choose this, then to run over there," I tell the audience as I pick DNA Enhancement. Admittedly, my narration has been getting a bit ragged. But I've now got more than a million followers. A *million* people are watching me. It's crazy. I never closed the chat window, and now it's so busy the messages blur by. I close it again. It's too distracting.

PICK ENHANCEMENT, the mainframe screen says.

- EAGLE (FLIGHT, SPEED)
- GORILLA (STRENGTH, AGILITY)
- TYRANNOSAUR (SIZE, ATTACK)
- TARDIGRADE (INVINCIBILITY)

"Gotta go with T. rex," says Zach.

"Eagle!" says Max. "I want to see an elephant fly!"

"No way. Tardigrade," says Noah.

"What the heck is a tardigrade?" Zach asks.

"It's a microscopic animal, also called a water bear," Noah explains. "It's practically unkillable. They've, like, survived volcanoes and arctic ice and even outer space. I think it means you take zero damage."

Do we have to get the Animal Planet lecture now? I wonder.

"Cool," says Zach.

"Be invincible," Noah tells me.

We hear yipping and banging outside the door. Vyrus is forcing his way back in. I don't take Noah's advice. I'm remembering the firefly I saved. Its last words were something about choosing. . . .

"Pick *something*," says Zach.

"It said *choose*, but not what!" I holler into the microphone.

"The firefly," I add, since nobody has any idea what I'm talking about.

"Pick anything!" All three of my buddies are shouting, and Zach is pounding on my shoulders. But I'm frozen, trying to puzzle out what the firefly would have told me if it had lived a moment longer.

Vyrus kicks the door in, sending the cabinets and chairs I stacked there clattering across the floor. The fox is on me, biting and clawing, draining my health. I flicker from the screen. The clock appears, counting down to my respawn.

"What happened?" Zach asks, stunned.

"Lucas hesitated," Noah says. "He probably lost."

• • •

But the game isn't over yet. I respawn in time to see the transformed, T. rex-enhanced fox gallop across the savanna, leaping and crashing through the barriers. I follow in his path of wreckage, back to the crossroads. He stops and is still. I stop too, reckoning that if I lost to pre-dinosaur-enhanced Cyrus, I'm not going to beat *this* thing.

"What's going on?" Max asks.

"Cyrus is using the potty?" Zach guesses.

Somewhere in the house a phone rings, and then Mom appears.

"Phone call for you," she whispers. "It's Cyrus."

"BRB AFK," I hurriedly tell the audience and step out in the hall. I don't know how Cyrus got our home number, but it doesn't matter.

"Hey," I say into the phone.

"Lukezilla!" he says. "This has been, without a doubt, the most epic game race ever." He sounds as tired as I feel. "I was thinking. You know, it's a team game. We can finish it together. We can both win. We can beat the game *together*."

"Seriously?"

"Since I'm about to win, I thought I'd offer that fig leaf," he says.

"Olive branch."

"What?" he asks tiredly.

"A peace offering is an olive branch, not a fig leaf," I explain, surprised that I'm able to retrieve such knowledge from my exhausted brain.

"What's a fig leaf then?"

"Something you use to hide your shame," I tell him. "Like trying to tie the game now because you played like a scrub. Let me take out all the opponents and then you sneak in for the prize."

"Whoa, whoa," he says. "I didn't cheat. I played the game by its rules."

Sure, I think. *Scrubs play by the rules too.*

"I didn't say you cheated," I tell him. Then, "Seriously, thanks for the offer. But I want to see if I can pull this off." I hang up and go back to the game. The Cyrannosaurus is still standing at attention. Maybe this time Cyrus really is taking a bathroom break. I give it a few minutes, thinking that it's unsporting to go on without him. But after fifteen minutes I decide I can't wait anymore.

"One more mission," I tell the world. "Let's go."

• • •

I didn't know then that the Steppe of Reckoning would go down as one of the toughest, most impossible, and grueling challenges in the history of video games, right up there with the Water Temple in *The Legend of Zelda: Ocarina of Time*, and the fight against the devil in *Cuphead* in expert mode. If you ask me, the Steppe of Reckoning is harder than either of those, because you can finish the water temple and the devil boss in a short amount of time if you know what you're doing. But even when you *do* know what you're doing, Reckoning is a slog, a marathon battle, one you can't rush. If you rush, you're done for.

The Pinchers amped up with tardigrade DNA are undefeatable unless you can pit them against one another, as I did. The tigress boss is the size of a T. rex and able to take down Trunkzilla with a single bite. The only way to get past her, if you're not amped yourself from the lab, is to lead her into a horde of her own boarlike minions. Which, if you remember, is a completely different area. It takes more than an hour to lure her there.

At around six, a new group arrives. Jacob, Nash, Lia, and Mia. They bring a stack of pizzas and a few big bottles of soda, and the lot of us eat in my room, me with a slice in my right hand and the WASD keys in my left. I've vanquished all the bosses, but must return yet again to the water tower with the explosives I got from the Steppe. Apparently, the tower is full of toxic gas, and releasing it will bring down the entire DNA-amped army.

At promptly nine o'clock, Dad enters the room and gives me a look. I look back with panicked, desperate eyes.

"We had a deal," he says.

"Dad, I need another hour! And I have ten million people watching!"

"Ten million?" He sighs. "Well, all right. One more hour."

It takes me fifty minutes. I detonate the explosives, and the monstrosities fall. There's a long cutscene with them gasping and dying.

"It's actually pretty sad," I tell the audience as we watch.

I find out later that if you've amped up your DNA, you die along with the mutants. The firefly—Lampyra—is there to warn you. Choose *nothing*. If Cyrus had finished the game, he'd have lost anyway. His Rexified fox disintegrates.

But I walk away unscathed. I've beaten the game.

"What's your favorite kind of tree?" I ask as the end credits roll.

The crowd behind me answers in a chorus. "THE VICK-TREE!"

"I do wonder what happened to Cyrus?" I say to the audience before I sign off. "I was expecting a final showdown."

We find out later that in his four-million-dollar home in Charlotte, North Carolina, Cyrus Papakagis fell asleep on the toilet.

CHAPTER 18

Cyrus's explanation is that he was still exhausted from the tour. Probably true, but he's ridiculed up and down the internet. The most circulated meme is his empty desk—which he broadcast *for hours*—with the caption SORRY, GUYS, I'M POOPED.

He turns it around by inventing a new bit. He says he's so excited he's going to—and then pretends to fall asleep. Which means he's dropped the stroke joke completely. "That was more played out than an Elvis record in a Memphis jukebox," he said in one video.

• • •

Max tells me he's sorry.

He says he was really sad that Tori's new team didn't make it to the finals in Chicago, and the team she started did. He also thought they had a better chance of winning if they were both on the team. That part might be true. They really play

229

well together. He also says that at first they thought since Zach didn't have a ride to Chicago, it might go perfectly, with her taking *his* place.

"Then you went and found him a ride," Max says with a sigh.

"Yeah, well, he was part of the team."

"Well, once that happened and you got memed, we kind of talked each other into thinking you had it coming," Max says. "Which is dumb, but that's what happened."

And now they're both banned for life and I have my account back. They still have their trophies, though. It'll have to do.

• • •

Cyrus and I trade private messages on Streamcast. He tells me how to monetize my Streamcast channel, which I can do since about a tenth of the ten million people who followed me through the mission became subscribers.

"I think you've got a real future in this, Lucas," he says. So, say what you want about Cyrus, he's not a sore loser.

• • •

But the bigger Streamcast story is Isaac. Seriously. Apparently, that executive I met at the tournament passed Isaac's book on to a new division that's developing original programming. It's not exactly a TV show and not exactly a game, but a kind of Choose-Your-Own-Adventure interactive story, like *Minecraft: Story Mode*. They have four programs coming, and one is based on Billie Ruth.

Yolanda tells me the news in October. I've dropped by during a day off school. Isaac is dozing in his favorite chair. He often does in the afternoon. I know Yolanda has been trying to find a place Isaac can live and get extra care, but it hasn't happened yet.

"The producer says they need to broaden their audience," Yolanda explains. "Right now they have millions of viewers, but they're all . . . uh . . ."

"Gamers and geeks?" I finish.

"Young males," she says. "That's what *the producer* said," she adds apologetically. "And all the other programs have white men as stars. They hope this will draw a whole new audience."

"Yeah, I've watched the sci-fi one they already launched," I tell Yolanda. "I'll definitely watch Isaac's."

"Me too," she says. "It's a godsend for Isaac. He retired a long time ago, and his money's been depleted. Now he can move somewhere nice."

"Hope it's somewhere close by," I say.

"Well, that's the thing," Yolanda says. "He's going to move into the same facility as his mother."

"In Chicago," I say, feeling a punch to my gut.

"They've been getting along better," she says. "I think it's best for both of them."

"Wow."

"We haven't told her about the program," Yolanda says. "Since it's not broadcast TV, she probably won't ever find out."

"Or maybe it'll be a big hit, and she'll finally appreciate it."

"Maybe," Yolanda says.

I sit there for a while, petting Petey. It's such great news for Isaac, but it's a lot to take in.

Isaac wakes up, sees me, and sits up straight. "Sorry, I didn't know we had company."

"I told him about your move," Yolanda says.

"It's true," he says after a moment. "Going to Chicago."

"I'm going to miss you," I tell him. "I'm going to miss eating olive sandwiches and listening to mysteries. And I'm going to miss this guy." I gently rub Petey's ear.

"Actually . . . ," he starts.

"What?"

"They won't let me have more than one pet. I'll take Sam. And I thought maybe you would want to take Petey. I know Petey would want to live with you. He doesn't like most people, but look at him."

Petey does look very content, sitting in my lap and purring.

"I would love that," I tell him. "I have to ask my parents." I remember I told them I'd never ask for anything ever again, but a cat in need of a home—and to help out Isaac—might be an exception.

• • •

Fortunately, Mom and Dad end up liking Petey as much as I do. Dad has to take allergy pills, but he says that's fine. Petey gets used to his new home fast. He sleeps on my bed and lays on the keyboard when I try to use the computer.

I'm counting down the days until winter break. I have a new team with Zach, Gabby, and one of her friends in Delaware, and we can't wait to hit the streets and smash noobs. I have a million followers on Streamcast waiting for my next video. My idea for the channel is to take a new account from scratch and see how fast I can get to level forty-five. I'm not sure how I'll battle and stream with a cat on the keyboard, but I expect Petey to be as big a star as I'm going to be.

ASSASSIN	CANNON
Vile (snake)	**Caprina** (ram)
Pincher (Dobermann)	**Crusher** (hyena)
Krawk (crocodile)	**Thorca** (hammerhead shark)
Shadow (panther)	**Minot** (bull)
Zigzap (electric eel)	**Pugiless** (kangaroo)
Ringo (red panda)	**Fumungus** (salamander)
Spry (monkey)	**Spike** (rhino)
Mustina (badger)	**Anthilla** (ant queen)
Burroughs (aardvark)	**Squunk** (skunk)
Leothrawl (lion)	**Kwill** (porcupine)
Saber (prehistoric tiger)	**Wyrm** (worm)

SUPPORT	TANK
Honeypie (bee)	Pango (pangolin)
Vigor (hummingbird)	Ursalot (brown bear)
Dracomiga (dragonfly)	Crusty (giant isopod)
Zikito (mosquito)	Buffle (bison)
Minerva (owl)	Cleo (giant beetle)
Bizzard (vulture)	Tortuga (turtle)
Pirrot (parrot)	Rutter (muskox)
Kathulopter (flying squid)	Isborg (polar bear)
Chiron (bat)	Gurrilla (gorilla)
Raptora (eagle)	Trunkzilla (elephant)
Lampyra (firefly)	Crankee (boar)

Photo by Andrew Karre

KURTiS SCALETTA has written books about sports, snakes, giant fungi, robots, bees, and video games. What connects them all is his interest in how kids handle tough moral choices. He lives in Minneapolis with his wife, son, and several cats. In addition to teaching and writing, he has saved the Kingdom of Hyrule more than a hundred times.